BIGFOOT IN THE BRONX

HUNTER SHEA

SEVERED PRESS
HOBART TASMANIA

BIGFOOT IN THE BRONX

Bigfoot was interviewed on The Patty Winters Show this morning and to my shock I found him surprisingly articulate and charming. – *American Psycho* by Bret Easton Ellis

"Ladies and gentlemen, the Bronx is burning." – Howard Cosell

For some damn good and funny people who, for some reason, are entertained by my cryptid fascination and haven't asked me to seek professional help…yet. That's right, I'm talking about you Steve Barnard and Sheridan Bradford. Also, to my super beta readers and friends, Kim Yerina and Janine Pipe. You're the best!

Now, let's get squatchy…

CHAPTER ONE

The heady scent of blood and shit were the first clues that something was wrong. Sheridan Barnard took a deep whiff as he stood on the top step leading to the door of his rotting RV. The mobile home's tires had long turned to flattened, flaking rubber, the old man's hidden abode canting at an angle that made walking within it akin to a jaunt down a tunnel while suffering from an inner ear infection.

Barnard cocked his head and held his breath, listening for something, anything, riding shotgun with the cool morning breeze. A hawk cried high overhead, circling around his plot of land.

"You know more than I do," Barnard mumbled to the sky. He stepped backward into the RV, closing the door slowly, quietly, cursing the rusty hinge that didn't give a whit about stealth.

He shivered, not so much from the cold, but the electric rush of adrenaline that raced through his veins. Tossing on a plaid hunting jacket that had more holes than a conspiracy theory, he grabbed his rifle from its place above the door, saw the reflection of his white bearded, crazy-eyed face in the browning mirror, and decided if he was going to do this, he might as well yank the bits of last night's franks and beans out of his scraggly scruff.

Stepping out of the RV, he took a deep breath and confirmed his assumption.

Death surrounded him.

The hawk was joined by another, the pair flying just a little lower, most likely praying to the bird gods that he would go the hell away.

Barnard followed the stench and the silence. It didn't take a rocket scientist to put two and two together on this one. He just hoped…

When the twig snapped under his foot, startling a chicken that had been cowering behind a bush, the dumb fowl got to clucking and screeching like its tail feathers were on fire. It scooted from its hiding place, scampering just feet from an equally surprised Sheridan Barnard. The old man reacted swiftly and without mercy, blasting the terrified chicken into a confetti of blood and stained feathers.

It took him a moment to realize what he'd done. His heart pulsed behind his Adam's apple.

"You stupid son of a bitch!" he said to the deceased chicken as much as to himself. A hearty dose of chicken blood splattered his jeans, not that it was easy to see it amidst the pre-existing patchwork of filth.

Something moved in the brush ahead, and from the heavy sound of it, he was pretty sure it wasn't another goddamn chicken.

Sucking in a reedy breath, Barnard ran to the sound.

"Kill my chickens," he shouted. "You better not choke on a bone before I get my crack at you!"

Barnard limp-stumbled down the zig-zagging path he'd trod down to the bare soil over his years of happy seclusion. The chicken coop was just around the bend under the shade of a pair of pussy willow trees. The closer he got, the worse the smell.

Just like that Toucan Sam used to tell you, old man, he thought. *Follow yer nose!*

He could feel the footfalls of another close by. It sounded as if they were coming from the other side of the coop and quickly getting away. Branches snapped up ahead with alarming frequency.

"You got greedy," Barnard blurted between heavy breaths. "Should have gone back to your hole before I woke up."

He turned the corner, the rifle stock steady in front of him like a bloodhound on the scent. The door to the coop had been torn off and was sitting atop a berry bush. Inside the tiny home was pure carnage. All of the chickens were dead, torn apart and tossed about. There were no heads to be seen. That hop-damn thing loved the heads.

When Barnard stopped to take in the chicken massacre, so had the retreating footfalls. His chest heaved and his old bones cried out for him to sit a spell.

"So much for eating well the next few months." Fall died fast up here and winters were a misery when you couldn't get to town and didn't have the cash to get anything even if some outsider who didn't shun you gave you a ride.

There, within that tangle of ripped wings, legs, burst breasts and enough plucked feathers to make one think they'd stumbled upon the aftermath of a Penthouse Letters sorority house pillow fight – albeit one with a little too much blood and gizzards – lay the remains of fresh eggs in the morning and beer can chicken at night.

"You're enjoying this, aren't you?" Barnard hissed in the direction of the heavy brush ahead. The morning sun had a hard time penetrating the dense foliage, but there were a few stray shafts poking through like light through a keyhole.

Barnard squinted into one of those keyholes.

Something moved. He was sure of it. The ray of light flashed off and back on.

"You might as well come on out and finish me off. After this, I'm good as dead come the cold weather. You can have me fresh, or break into my RV and lick me like a grizzled popsicle later."

As much as he wanted to scream and rant and curse, his cooler side prevailed.

Just soft talk it on out of there. A little bit closer is all I need.

A rock the size of his palm came sailing out of the brush. It hit the top of the coop with a loud crack and tumbled well away from Barnard. It almost made him pull the trigger. He tried to settle his nerves but that seemed about as impossible as time travel in a cardboard box.

"I'm not gonna hurt you," he said as soothingly as he could. "I know I interrupted your breakfast. But even you should know I had a right to be angry. That's my breakfast, too. A whole shit ton of them. You wanna finish?" He took three steps back, his eyes never leaving that pinhole of light. This was the closest he'd ever come and the maddest he'd ever been. He may not get this chance again. Lord knows, he wouldn't have the chickens to entice the bastard anymore.

He bent down, lifted up a bird carcass and flipped it over the coop, toward the edge of the tree line. "There you go."

The breeze ruffled the low hanging limbs of the pussy willow trees. It reminded Barnard of the leather straps that hung down from the car wash he used to work at. All those things did was spread the dirt around.

Another stone, this one smaller, plunked the grass to Barnard's left.

"Only sissies throw rocks."

A quick, soft huff replied back. It could have been a gust of wind winding down the throat of the trees, but Barnard knew better.

"My grandma farted louder and meaner than that. If you mean to scare me off, it'll take a whole lot more than a pebble and a grunt." The wind shifted, carrying with it an eye-rolling perfume of wet animal and rotten musk. He wasn't sure if it was an improvement over the chicken crap and guts. "Now come on, I'm meaning to make peace with you. Ain't you got no manners?"

Maybe it knew about guns and was smart enough to keep its distance. Well, it was too late to hide the rifle. Besides, where was Barnard going to put it anyway? Up his keister?

The creature rattled some low hanging limbs and barked like a sick dog. It made Barnard's gonads seek higher ground, but he wasn't going to let *it* know that.

"Come on now. Breakfast is getting cold and so am I."

He saw a blur of movement and slipped his finger over the trigger. The creature had shifted to another vantage point, one that was as dark as the ass end of a deep well.

Maybe it was smarter than he was giving it credit for.

Barnard shifted his position so he was facing in the general direction of where he thought the chicken killer hid. He took several more steps back until he was almost at the bend and out of sight of the carnage. It was as far as he could go. If the thing was too cautious to come any further, Barnard figured he'd just start blasting. With his nearest neighbor miles away and it being hunting season, a few cracks in the morning would draw as much attention as a chirping chickadee.

As much as he wanted to goad it into action, there was a chance his running mouth wasn't doing him any favors.

Would you please shut that trap of yours. I swear, that mouth could swallow a train, his mother used to say. He'd spent the first half of his life talking a blue streak and the second out here with no one to jaw at.

I'm shutting up, mom, he thought, his lips mouthing the words.

Stillness settled around the man and hidden beast.

Barnard's limbs tingled, his breath coming in short, shallow gasps.

If things went tits up, no one would hear him scream.

There was sudden movement in the brush. It seemed to come from everywhere. He raised his rifle, trying in vain to track the source of the commotion.

"Oh shit."

His finger took action before his brain could tell it to stop. It pulled the trigger, the shot going into the pussy willow trees. There was no sound of it hitting anything. It just sailed into the morning sky.

The tree to his left swayed.

Barnard took another shot.

Now the tree to his right shook to its roots, as if it had been struck by a Mac Truck. He fired wildly, hoping that if none of his shots hit home, they would at least discourage the beast from making any more sudden moves.

The creature let loose with a monkey-like whoop, followed by a low, rumbling growl that made Barnard mess himself.

It was time to run.

As he spun on his heels, it burst from the tree, descending on him like the hairy hammer of God.

There was no time to lift his rifle and shoot.

There was no time to scream.

There was no time to…

CHAPTER TWO

Shay Walsh checked his pack, added a little more ice to the cooler and set his gun bag on the kitchen counter. He took a sip of too-hot coffee and fanned his open mouth. "Jesus, that's hot. Are you trying to kill me?"

His wife Katie shook her head and settled her elbows on the counter, both hands cradling a mug, wisps of steam rising from its surface. Her bed-head of tousled dirty blonde locks made Shay wish he had time to whisk her back to the bedroom. "I just took it off the stove. What did you think it was going to be? You're lucky I even made it. You know how much I hate getting up early when I don't have to."

"And for that, a set of wings have been set aside in Heaven with your name on them." Shay leaned over the counter and kissed the tip of her nose. Katie was a nurse at Montefiore Hospital and had been pulling double shifts so they could pay the bills. Shay's unemployment checks had run dry a month ago and his resume wasn't getting so much as a nibble.

"Being married to a devil like yourself better guarantee my wings," she said with a smile that lit up her tired eyes. "Promise me you won't drink too much and get yourselves shot, eh?"

He hefted the cooler. "I didn't pack enough for even one of us to get the slightest bit fluthered. Just enough to wet our whistles."

"The great hunters of Woodlawn," Katie said, raising a fist. "And not a deer was the least bit worried."

"Har, har. This is the year, honey. I had a dream about it the other night." He took a deep breath. "Can you smell it?"

Katie raised an eyebrow. "Smell what?"

"I believe it's venison with garlic butter and thyme, sizzling on the grill. What do you want on the side?"

"My husband with no extra holes in him."

He put a hand over his heart. "Woman, you wound my pride."

"And you're keeping me awake. Now, off you go. I'm sure Vito is already in the truck waiting for you. Remember, tomorrow is Halloween and Caitlin wants you to take her trick or treating. That means come back in one piece and *not* hungover."

He gathered his things and leaned in for a proper kiss. "While I'm gone, you should look up how to make deer jerky."

"I'll be sure to get right on that."

Shay grinned. "Don't you ever lose your sarcasm. Love you."

"Love you too, Hemingway."

He stepped onto the porch, the cold morning air waking him quicker than any cup of coffee. Katie waved and locked the door behind him.

He wasn't kidding about the dream. In it, he and Vito had each scored a buck that would feed them for months. Lord knows, Shay needed it. He and Katie and Caitlin had been existing on pasta and beans for what felt like months. A nice deer would do them both a world of good.

Sure, they'd come home empty handed for the past six years, but something felt different this year.

"Lucky number seven," he said, his breath curling over his face as he bounded down the cement steps to Vito's idling truck.

It was like being hit by the exhaust from a blast furnace when he opened the door.

"You really can't be that cold," Shay said, settling into his seat and buckling up.

Vito Esposito was his next door neighbor and friend since they had both peed their paints in kindergarten when Ms. Garten read them the picture book *What's Under My Bed*. As Vito liked to say, "Bonded by piss and full of shit. Our friendship has been in the toilet since day one."

Vito pulled the Ram truck away from the curb and barreled down the dark, narrow street. There was barely room for the Dodge, the side view mirrors nearly clipping the rows of cars parked on each side in unbroken rows. They passed by blocks of two family houses and one low-rise apartment building.

Shay had lived in that building until he was ten and his parents moved down the street next to Vito's family.

"It's gonna be colder than a meat locker up there," Vito said. He ran a hand over his shaved head. "Enjoy the heat while you can."

"If I don't melt or pass out."

They cruised over to Katonah Avenue, the main thoroughfare for their little slice of the Bronx. It was home to several good Irish pubs, three pizza parlors, a library that was the runt of the New York Public Library litter, German bakery, stationery store and the local public elementary school. At this time of morning, the bars were closed and the streets were empty. Only Nuala's Café was open, the light in the window warm and inviting. Vito double-parked and hopped out, coming back five minutes later with four bacon, egg and cheese sandwiches and coffee.

"Cheers," Vito said. They tapped sandwiches. "I'm mixing things up this year. I think it'll change our luck."

Shay took a big bite, the egg and cheese piping hot and spiced with pepper and a dash of ketchup. "Oh yeah? You bringing a heat seeking missile?"

It was no secret that Vito was a terrible shot. His eyes got worse each year, but the stubborn guy refused to get glasses. Shay wasn't much better, which accounted for some of why they would never be confused with big game hunters. In the past, these trips were really just about getting away to the country and escaping from the grind of everyday life.

This year was different for Shay. And he knew Vito was hurting too, now that his hours had been cut at the Parks and Rec Department. Maybe that's why he was trying something different. Anything to flip their luck to the good side of the coin.

"Care to tell me what it is?"

Vito eased onto the Bronx River Parkway, heading north. "It's a surprise. How happy are you that they moved the game to the afternoon?"

Their daughters were on the same youth soccer team, a sport that attracted crazed sports parents like termites to a wood pile in their corner of the Bronx. The Irish from the other side, as they referred to the majority of the population that had been immigrating to the area for as long as anyone could remember, took soccer insanely serious, even when it was a game with nine-year-olds running up and down the field. The Walsh and Esposito families were not the norm.

"Our team is so terrible, it would be nice if they just forfeit. Caitlin cries before every game."

Vito chuckled. "Meredith curses a blue streak. I don't know which one I'd prefer."

They settled into a comfortable silence and Shay fell asleep by the time they rolled onto the Mario Cuomo Bridge, heading up to what the pair of city boys considered the wilds of Ulster County.

An hour and a half later, Shay came to when Vito backhanded him on the chest.

"We're almost there, Sleeping Beauty."

Shay rubbed his eyes and looked out the window. They were driving on a narrow two-lane road, the first rays of sunlight just starting to peek over the mountain ahead of them.

"Sorry about that," Shay said, downing the cold coffee Vito had brought from Nuala's.

The radio was tuned to a sports talk station, the host bemoaning the lowly state of the Jets, which was an annual whine fest for their beleaguered fans.

"You're turning into an old man," Vito said, laughing. "Or a baby in a car seat. Though you're too damn ugly to be a baby."

"You ever see your baby pictures?"

They passed a sign for the Peaceful Valley Resort ten miles ahead. The old resort had a passing resemblance to the Overlook Hotel in *The Shining*. Once a jewel of the Catskills, it had fallen into disrepair, which made it a cheap place to take the families for New Year's Eve. The restaurant had decent food and it was BYOB for the cigar bar and lounge. There were activities for the kids and it all capped off with a party in the old club as the ball dropped. If they were lucky, there was snow on the ground and the next day would be spent watching *The Honeymooners* marathon and going out sledding.

It was something they all looked forward to until the year the whole place had been taken over by what they had assumed was some kind of Eastern European crime syndicate and their families. The revelry resulted in shouting, punching, flowing vodka and Shay was sure he heard gunshots outside their room at three in the morning. That had been the last of the trips to The Peaceful Valley Resort.

Between yawns, Shay said, "I don't know, I've just been exhausted lately."

He knew exactly why. He was depressed, his anxiety from being jobless dragging him into lethargy instead of lighting a fire under his ass.

Vito rolled the windows down and let a flood of startlingly crisp air wash over them. Shay was instantly awake. Vito was quick to put the windows back up. "See, now you're up."

"And I'll stay that way. I'm afraid if I doze off again, you'll take ice from the cooler and scoop it onto my nuts."

"That would never happen," Vito took a hard right, "because you don't have nuts."

"I'd rather that than all beans and no pole like some people in this car."

"I fly my flag just fine. Danielle salutes every time with a smile."

"You always confuse smiling with grimacing."

Shay thought about the cold bottles of Heineken in the cooler and wondered if it was too early to have one. It was just him and Vito and the great outdoors. Who would know or care?

His guilty conscience would know, that's who. He'd been drinking more and earlier in the day over the past couple of months. Drinking cost money, money they couldn't spare. So far, Katie hadn't said a word about it, just the occasional look that told him she was getting concerned.

Vito went on his usual rant on why Shay should abandon the Jets and jump on the Giants bandwagon. Normally, Shay would be up for the verbal sparring match. He needed something warm and familiar to get him out of his funk. It just wasn't cutting through.

The entrance for the Minnewaska State Park was illuminated by the truck's headlights. Shay felt a little shiver of anticipation.

For once, shoot like you don't need binoculars for glasses.

They passed the entrance and continued down what passed for a road. Ten shock-absorbing minutes later, Vito pulled the truck into a gravel lot tucked behind an abandoned house that was off the beaten path. They had found it several years earlier and knew it was a good place to enter the park without having to worry about a Park Ranger confiscating their beer. They could just as easily have gone into the park like normal people, but Vito wasn't happy unless he was bending a rule. He always *had a guy* or *knew a place.*

"Let's go kill some Bambis," Vito said, hopping out.

"You don't have to put it that way," Shay said, removing his gear from the Ram.

"Oh, right. It was Bambi's mom they killed. My bad."

Bambi had been Caitlin's favorite movie for a good year when she was five. He wished Vito had chosen something else. Anything but *Deliverance.*

Vito removed a strange looking bag from the covered flatbed.

"What on Earth do you have there?" Shay asked. He fastened his ball cap on his head and raised his coat collar. It must have been twenty degrees colder out here.

His friend unzipped the bag. "Whaddya think?" He held the bow over his head like the cover of that old Conan movie poster.

"You're going to try your hand at bow hunting?"

"Yeah. I bought it when Danielle and I went to the casino in the Poconos over the summer. I even took some lessons while we were there. The instructor said I was pretty good."

Shay rolled his eyes. "That's because he wanted to get paid. Bow hunting is like a hundred times harder, you know. And last time I checked, you ain't Rambo."

"We'll see," Vito replied with a boyish grin. The man could not resist new toys and he looked so pleased with himself, Shay bit his tongue.

They stood side-by-side, staring into the distant trees, the cool mountain air alive with the aroma of fall leaves and pine.

"Ladies first," Vito said, sweeping his hand toward the trail leading into the woods.

Shay walked past him. "And little girls second."

Vito clapped him on his shoulder and gave it a squeeze. The pair of lifetime buddies headed into the slice of wilderness.

"I know how much you need this, bud," Vito said. "I swear, this is the year. We're overdue."

Shay listened to the clinking bottle of beer in the cooler and his mouth watered just a bit.

CHAPTER THREE

After trekking for a mile or so, they stopped for a rest and to apply scent block so any potential deer wouldn't detect them. The key now was to find a place to hunker down for the shank of the day, lying low and keeping downwind so they blended in with the environment as best they could.

"Here comes my favorite part," Shay said.

"What's that?"

"When you have to keep your mouth shut for hours."

"Keep yours closed tight, buddy. It smells like something died in your stomach."

"Must have been those liver fajitas your mother made me."

They sputtered with controlled laughter. Nearly forty and they still interacted like teenagers. Vito appreciated that about Shay. Even though he had gone the route of the white collar worker, he'd never forgotten his blue collar roots. Vito just wished he could find a job for his friend and get him out of his funk. He'd given Katie a grand the previous month, with strict instructions not to tell Shay. It pained her to lie to her husband, but even she knew it was for the best. They needed the money and Shay didn't need any more guilt.

Vito had a bottle of deer urine and sprayed it on the bottoms of their boots. It wasn't exactly potpourri, but deer had an incredible sense of smell and would smoke out a pair of dopey humans a mile away. They walked the rest of the way in silence, taking care to avoid stepping on twigs and crunchy leaves as much as possible.

Shay held up a hand, military style (though the closest they ever got to the military was watching *The Hurt Locker* a dozen times together) and signaled to a primo spot for them to settle in. A pair of three-foot high rocks were nestled against two trees that were spaced about ten feet apart. Beyond them was a small, open field.

Vito gave him a thumbs-up. It was as if fate had set this spot up just for them. Shay took the furthest big rock while

Vito hunkered down, but not before Shay had tossed him a beer. Vito tucked the beer under his shirt to open it, muffling any sound. He took a sip and winced from the cold.

Now came the boring part. Sitting and waiting for hours. They weren't even guaranteed to see a deer, much less bag one. More times than most, they returned from their foray into the woods having only spotted some squirrels and a chipmunk.

Offering a silent prayer while touching the Saint Christopher medal he'd worn around his neck since his grandmother had given it to him for his grammar school graduation, Vito checked the wind to make sure it hadn't shifted.

Man, this was a good location. He carefully laid out several arrows on the ground within easy reach. Not that he thought he'd ever have time for a second shot.

He promised himself that if they did manage to bring a deer home, the lion's share would go to Shay. Vito would be happy with some meat for deer chili and maybe a couple of steaks.

Silence had never been his strong suit, making this vigil exceedingly difficult. He wanted to tell Shay about the pair of wrinklies he'd found going at it in the park bathroom the other day. The sight, and sounds, still disturbed him. Who knew grandparents liked to fuck in public places, if at all! He figured the only way to exorcise that demon was to put it in Shay's head. It would have to wait until the walk back to the truck.

The woods had been silent on their arrival, but after a time, the critters returned to their daily rituals, forgetting that a pair of humans were in their midst. Vito hoped the same went for the deer.

He'd tracked the activity to this place a week ago. Always follow the game trail. We weren't so different from one another.

Sheridan Barnard munched on an old, stale biscuit, his keen eyes never leaving the field. A couple of hours ago, he'd spotted some birds lighting off the trees across the way, headed in his direction. He'd gotten his hopes up, but hope died hard and fast.

I'll wait here all damn day and into the night, he thought. *Not like I have anything else to do. You messed with the wrong man, you big, bitchin' bastard.*

He rubbed the knot that was still on the back of his head going on two weeks now. That damn thing had cold-cocked him good from behind, like a coward. Barnard had been out for a few minutes, and saw stars for the rest of the day. Once his head cleared, his focus narrowed to a laser beam. Payback was a bitch, just like all his exes.

It would be nice to be in his lounger that he'd found on the curb outside someone's house five years ago. It would be nicer to be in said lounger with a full belly. Instead, he was out here, on high alert, cold, starved and madder than a pet raccoon.

His fingers tightened around his rifle until the pain in his knuckles told him to take a breath.

It was going to be a half moon tonight. Plenty of light to see by, if need be.

No, Barnard wasn't going anywhere.

Vito had fallen asleep. When he came to, he hoped he hadn't been snoring. He looked to Shay. His friend looked back and smiled, mouthing, *take a nice nap, grandpa?*

Clearing drool on his chin with his sleeve, he peeked over the rock and out onto the field. Empty. He checked his watch. It was almost 3:30. Getting close to prime time. Vito flexed his fingers, knocking out the rust. He sure could use a beer, but he didn't dare move or ask Shay to chuck one over, hoping Vito would catch it.

Beer is for closers.

It they were going to bag a deer, these next couple of hours held all of their hope. The sun would set around 4:20 (he'd checked his phone before they'd left the neighborhood).

He stared into the field and the trees around it, waiting for the slightest bit of movement. His ears were cocked, ready to catch any sound carried on the pre-dusk breeze.

His stomach grumbled but it would have to wait. Opening up something to eat would telegraph they were here to any deer in the area. Vito couldn't help thinking of an eggplant parm wedge from Tony's Pizza. The gurgling in his stomach threatened to give away their position.

Shay must have heard it, because he shook his head disapprovingly at Vito.

Vito flipped him the bird and changed his thoughts to his mother-in-law's meatloaf. That would kill any appetite. Momma Nancy had two fat dogs that could barely walk. Vito estimated that half their body weight came from hunks of that awful meatloaf being surreptitiously dropped to the floor during family dinners.

Now he thought about the bet he'd made on today's Giants game. Kickoff would be soon. They would listen to it in the truck on the way home. Maybe they could pick it up at halftime. If the Giants covered the spread, he was set to make four hundred bucks. First thing he'd buy was an eggplant parm wedge.

And now his stomach grumbled again. Vito pressed a fist into his gut, as if to threaten it with physical violence if it didn't cut out the racket it was making.

He was about to mouth an apology to Shay when he saw his friend's gaze was locked onto something in the distance. Vito turned to see what Shay was looking at.

Holy shit!

It was a deer. A four-point buck to be exact. It walked slowly into the field, its nose to the ground, munching on the dry grass.

Vito held his breath.

Come this way, buddy. Just need you about twenty-five yards closer.

He didn't touch his bow. Not yet. It was too soon and he didn't want to spook the buck. Shay had his hand on the barrel of his propped rifle, but he was as immobile as a statue.

In the past, this is the time when one of them would do something stupid and chase the deer away. Not that it mattered. Just being out here had been good enough for them.

Today, it mattered.

Breathing slowly through his mouth, Vito stared at the buck, willing it to come to them. They had a clear sight line. It was just a matter of time. The buck continued to graze, unconcerned that it was in the sights of two predators.

Suddenly, the deer's head jerked up, ears twitching.

Vito ground his teeth.

Fuck! What did we do this time?

He cast a quick glance at Shay. His friend shrugged his shoulders. It could have been something as simple as a squirrel dropping an acorn from a tree. Deer were normally skittish, but more so this time of year. They were smarter than people gave them credit for. They knew there were killers amongst them.

The buck's hind legs tensed for a moment, and then it was sprinting across the field.

And miracle of miracles, it was heading straight for them!

Shay lifted his rifle just as Vito notched an arrow in his bow. No worries about being quiet now. The deer's mad dash would cover any sound they made.

Vito had never tried using his bow and arrow on a moving target before. Maybe he'd get lucky. Truth be told, Shay had the better chance, but Vito would never tell him that.

Sweat slipped into Vito's left eye. The deer was almost in range. He locked gazes with the animal. Its orbs were wide and dark and panicked.

Just a little closer.

A brown blur caught Vito's attention form the periphery of his vision. It was racing toward the deer with the speed of a cheetah.

What the hell is that?

The buck momentarily forgotten, Vito tried to reconcile what he was seeing. Was it a bear? Sure, they walked on two legs, but the key word was *walked*. They didn't run like an Olympian on a speed-steroid cocktail.

The upright, sprinting animal was headed for the buck.

Vito turned to Shay. His friend had let his rifle point to the ground. He watched the scene play out in stunned silence.

The animal closed the distance in seconds. It leapt at the buck, massively long, hairy arms outstretched like a defensive end blanketing a quarterback. Vito should know. He'd watched the Giants' crappy O-line allow any and all defenders hammer the franchise QB for the past two seasons.

With a wild, terrified shriek, the buck was tackled to the ground, stopped dead under the weight of the…of the…

Vito rocked back on his heels as the creature dove head-first into the buck's neck, burrowing into fur and flesh. When it pulled its head away, Vito swore it did so to look straight at him.

Holy freaking shit! The bow shook in Vito's hands.

The face looking at him was neither animal nor man. It was an amalgam of both, its tanned face looking like worn leather, huge, black eyes under a bony, jutting brow, the only part of its being not covered in what looked like long, coarse hair. Blood dripped down its chin and onto its chest.

This was no escaped gorilla from a zoo – not that there were any zoos up this way. And it wasn't a man in a costume. First, no man could run that fast. Second, Vito had field dressed a few deer, and he couldn't imagine the strength it would take to rip out a chunk of a deer's neck like that. Their hides required a knife so sharp, it could cut your balls off without you even knowing it happened.

"What the fuck is it?" he called over to Shay. There was no sense pretending the creature didn't know they were there. It bared its fangs. This close, Vito could see a dangling strip of flesh hanging from one of its incisors.

"I…I don't know." Shay lifted his rifle again.

The creature, never taking its eyes from where Vito and Shay were hiding, stood up, one foot on the deer's ruined neck, the other on the ground. It puffed out its chest and sent a series of deep, guttural barks their way, as if to say, *you have five seconds to leave before I do to you what I did to this buck.*

It took a menacing step toward them.

Vito pulled back on the bow. When the creature took another step, his nervous fingers lost their grip. An arrow sailed pathetically away, nowhere near the monster.

He fumbled to snatch another arrow, fearing taking his eyes from the approaching beast.

"Shay, you got it in your sights?" he shouted, hearing the tremor in his voice.

Shay didn't answer.

"Dude, shoot the fucking thing."

Shay was frozen and silent.

Vito had finally gotten a grip on an arrow when he heard an echoing *ka-pow, ka-pow!*

The creature stopped, its eyes gone big and round as silver dollars. One of its hands reached for its back.

Vito's second arrow went straight into the sky, sailing harmlessly away. Shay finally fired his rifle. Vito couldn't tell where the bullet went, but he was pretty sure it was nowhere near the monster.

And that's when he saw another figure running away. It was most definitely a man. He must have crept up when their full attention was on the grisly nature display of something completely unnatural.

Now the creature wobbled, its mouth gone slack.

Its left leg bent hard at the knee, and then the right followed. The creature let out a piteous sound a moment before face planting into the dirt. There, Vito saw what looked like two darts sticking up from its fur-matted back. The man that shot the creature slipped into the trees across the field.

Vito walked on equally unsteady legs to Shay. Shay had to hold onto the rock to keep upright.

"Jesus Christ, can you believe this?" Vito exclaimed. He was starting to hyperventilate. "I mean, what the hell just happened? What is that thing?"

Shay rested his rifle against the rock and chewed on his thumbnail. He looked like someone who'd been hypnotized, his mind a million miles away.

"We better get the hell out of here before that thing wakes up," Vito said. He did not want to end up like the buck.

When Shay didn't respond, Vito grabbed him by the arm. "Come on, man. We gotta go."

Shay spit out a crescent of nail and swallowed hard and loud. "We're not leaving it here."

"Take a picture if you want, but we have to get the fuck outta here. You saw what it can do. If it wakes up, we can't outrun it. And our necks are a hell of a lot easier to tear open. Right now, I'd give anything to be at Meredith's soccer game."

Shay shushed him by fanning his hand up and down. "Take a breath. Okay? We can't just run away like a couple of scared children. Not from this."

Vito was about to correct him and say they were going to run like a couple of scared adults when Shay said, "We have proof of Bigfoot right in front of us. We're going to be rich!"

CHAPTER FOUR

Sheridan Barnard leaned against a tree and tried to catch his breath. His hand was over his chest, feeling the banging of his heart like it was trying out for a part in that Poe story he'd been forced to read in high school. Not venturing too far from the field, he just needed a place to take cover. It was the logical thing to do when one was shot at.

Not that he could be sure he was the intended target. Whoever had pulled the trigger was naturally scared. Who wouldn't be after seeing such a thing? Barnard wasn't going to take any chances. He nailed that son of a bitch good with those tranquilizer darts.

The rifle and darts were the remnants of his time working at the old Catskill Game Farm, a shoddy zoo that had seen better days by the time he'd started there as a glorified shit shoveler. They had everything from giraffes to tigers, baboons to a giant rat called a capybara. Thing was as nasty as his ex-wife Linda was mean. The cages and enclosures had been in much disrepair. It was a miracle none of the paying visitors got hurt there, aside from a nip or two from the goat and sheep feeding/petting zone.

Barnard had snatched the rifle when the place was in the process of shutting down for good.

He wasn't sure the chemicals in the darts would still work after all this time, even though he'd kept them in his fridge for some odd reason.

Life is strange. It takes you where it wants you to go.

His big plan was to knock the bigfoot out and drag it home so he could alert the authorities. Some zoo or government agency would take the chicken killer off his hands and he'd get some fame and maybe much needed cash to boot.

Settling himself down, Barnard watched and waited. Hopefully, whoever had shot at him was hightailing it out of the forest. If not, there might be a problem.

Shay handed his rifle to Vito and said, "Watch my back."

"Dude, really?"

Shay crept forward, making his way to the fallen bigfoot. That's what it had to be, right? The closer he got, the more sure of it he was. Bears didn't look like this. Gorillas didn't either. It had to be almost seven feet tall and about three hundred pounds. Maybe more, since it looked pretty muscular. He took out his phone, his jittery, clumsy fingers having a hard time swiping to get to the camera app.

"Vito, you have to see this."

The smell hit him like a hammer to the septum. It was a stench so thick, it left a film on Shay's tongue.

His steps hurried as he got closer. He let the video roll as he walked around the fallen creature. The bottoms of its feet were nearly black and had the texture of old baseball mitts. Shay clicked photos as he recorded. His brain was on fire, which was a welcome distraction from the stench.

"It's a fucking sasquatch," he murmured. Then he looked to Vito and shouted, "I was right! It is a bigfoot. Come here."

Vito looked uneasy. Shay worried that if the thing moved, Vito's understandably unsteady hands would leave Shay the victim of friendly fire.

"Seriously. You have to see it." Shay popped down to his haunches and stared at the bigfoot's back. It didn't rise and fall. "I think it's dead."

"You took your video, now let's go," Vito said.

"Video won't be enough. People can fake anything." He thought of looking for a pulse, but the beast had no discernable neck. Not that he really wanted to touch it.

Twigs crunched behind Shay.

"I should just shoot it in the head to be sure," Vito said.

Shay turned on him. "Are you crazy? You'll destroy the evidence."

Vito looked beyond the fallen monster to the opposite trees. "What about the guy who shot it? I'm sure he'll come back for it."

"Over my dead body, he will."

"Have you lost your mind?"

Shay looked at the bigfoot. His brain buzzed as much as the gathering flies. "Maybe. But maybe this is the one thing that can change our lives."

"Trust me, my life is changed, bro. I'm never going in the woods again and I'm never going to laugh at those bigfoot shows."

"You think you can bring the truck here?"

"What?"

"It's too damn big to carry out. Our hearts would pop before we got twenty feet."

Vito waved a fly away and cringed. "I'm not putting that thing in my truck."

"It'll be in the flatbed. I'll clean it out later. And we can spray it with that no scent stuff. It might cut through the funk."

"No. Not happening."

Shay appealed to his friend. "This thing right here, it's more than a bigfoot. It's paying off the mortgage to your house. It's Meredith's college fund. It's that trip to Bora Bora Danielle and Katie always talk about us taking but know we'd never be able to afford. It's a whole new life for us. Lord knows, the old one is in need of a kick in the ass."

Vito closed his eyes and took a deep breath. "This is insane."

"I know it is. That's what makes it invaluable."

Vita paced in a tight circle. Shay could see the inner turmoil playing out on his face.

"What if it's not dead?" Vito said. "You want to die out here? Or better yet, on the New York State Thruway?"

Shay wanted, no, *needed* his friend to come around to his way of thinking. There could be only one way to do that. "You don't think it's dead? Here, I'll prove it."

His skin crawled as he reached out to touch the fallen beast. If he was being honest, a large part of him worried that Vito was right. Flight was battling mightily with fight.

You do this and Katie can finally take a much needed break. Hell, she may even be able to quit that job. You could make all of her dreams come true.

Sucking in a great gulp of air, he thrust his hand out until it settled on the bigfoot's back. Vito stepped aside and pointed Shay's rifle at the creature's head.

Nothing.

Its hair was rough as wool. Shay could feel its massive musculature underneath the thick, shaggy coat. What he didn't feel was any movement of even slight gurgling in its lungs.

Against his better judgment, he started to shake the beast very much the way he'd attempt to wake Caitlin when it was time to get up from school.

"Wakey, wakey."

"Dude, cut the shit."

Shay looked at Vito. "You wanted to know." He shook it harder. The heavy body barely moved.

"All right, next test."

Shay stood up and wiped his hand on his jeans. His skin felt oily, as if the sasquatch had some weird kind of secretion on its coat.

This is for you, Katie and Caitlin.

He pulled his foot back, hesitated just a moment, and proceeded to kick the bigfoot as hard as he could in its side. His toes slammed into the tip of his boot and sent ripples of hot pain through his foot and up his leg.

But the bigfoot didn't react.

With his heart racing and the back of his brain sending out a 'hallelujah, I'm not dead!', Shay smiled at Vito. "See? Stick in the fork, this guy's done. Now please, can you get the truck so we can get rich?"

The air of tension that had puffed Vito up started to release and he lowered the rifle. "We must be out of our minds, man."

"Nothing new there, buddy."

Vito looked around and handed the rifle back to Shay. "I hope you're not going to need this while I'm gone."

Feeling more confident, Shay put a foot on the bigfoot's back as if he were posing for his trophy photo. "I don't think he's going to give me any problems."

Staring into the woods beyond the field, Vito said, "No, I mean the person who OD'd this thing."

"You said he was running away. Let's hope he's gone wee-wee-wee, all the way home. The faster you get the truck, the quicker we're out of here and away from whoever the shooter is."

With his hands clasped over his head, Vito said, "Fine. If you need to, shoot to frighten, not to kill. You can't spend your bigfoot money in jail."

"I'm a lover, not a fighter. No humans will be harmed in the making of this fortune."

"Fine. I'll be back as fast as I can. That is, if I don't get lost."

It was going to be dark sooner than either of them would like. Vito took off at a healthy trot, leaping over a fallen log and disappearing into the woods.

Shay cast a way glance at the trees opposite him and the bigfoot corpse, and then went to get his cooler. His nerves were on fire, a deadly mix of fear and excitement that had him on emotional overload. There was only one way to settle down.

"Thank you, Jesus," he said, popping off the cap and downing a Heineken in two gulps.

Sheridan Barnard waited until dusk just to be safe. Stepping out of his hiding place, he looked through his binoculars and hissed a stream of curses. A truck was now in the field. He could see two men struggling to lift the bigfoot into the flatbed. They took turns stepping away and unleashing a torrent of vomit into the grass.

Serves them right, he thought. *It's not theirs to take!*

He could rush over there and try to chase them off. He had two more tranquilizer darts left, one for each squatch thief.

Problem was, it looked like the stuff in those darts was mighty powerful. The bigfoot looked more dead than asleep, especially considering the amount of time that had passed. Barnard may have been what the townies called him, a crazy coot, but he wasn't a killer. At least not of men.

Besides, they looked to be half his age and outnumbered him. Betting on those kinds of odds was the reason he'd drained his bank account three times during his second and next to last marriage.

They finally got the chicken killer in the flatbed and covered it with the hard top. Both men leaned against the tailgate, hands on their knees, heads bent, panting. It was getting too dark to make out details now, but it looked like they grabbed a couple of bottles of something and clinked them together.

"Congratu-fucking-lations," Barnard said. "You just robbed another man. Hope that thing stinks up your truck so you have to junk it. Assholes."

He stayed until they got in the truck, seething all the while.

As the moon dominated the night sky, billions of twinkling points splashing over the horizon, he did think there was a silver lining in all of this.

At least the damn thing was gone. It wouldn't bedevil him anymore. Small consolation, but like everything in Barnard's life, it was the best he could hope for. He slipped the rifle's strap over his shoulder and made the long walk back to his trailer, wondering if he could panhandle enough cash to buy some more chickens.

CHAPTER FIVE

The drive back home was not without its difficulties. Vito's arms trembled from exhaustion, exertion and the jittery wake from the receding waves of adrenaline. Shay polished off the beers in quick order and was in high spirits. There was one major problem that vexed Vito.

They smelled like the ass end of a sick coyote.

Even with the windows down and the cold air streaming in as they went over seventy miles-per-hour on the thruway, there was no eradicating the horrible funk of the dead bigfoot on their clothes and hands.

"I can't take this anymore," Vito said after sticking his head out of the window, the biting wind making his eyes water and bones quake.

"I don't know, I think I'm starting to get used to it," Shay said.

"That's because you're seven beers in, you crazy donkey."

"Hey, if someone is going to be the designated driver, that means someone has to step up and be the designated drinker."

Vito spied a sign for an exit two miles ahead. He remembered there being some strip malls and restaurants around that area.

"You might want to save a little for the champagne you said we'll be popping tomorrow," Vito said, nudging the gas pedal a little more to get off the highway as quickly as possible.

"There's always room for more." Shay picked the cooler up from its spot between his feet, opened the lid and rooted around, ice and bottles banging against one another. "Although in this case, there isn't more. We have a crisis."

Vito groaned inwardly. "Yeah, I know. We have a dead whatddayacallit in my truck."

"Cryptid."

"Whatever. How do you even know such a thing?"

"I've had a lot of time on my hands. Time wasted spent watching cable TV. You wouldn't believe how many shows there are on bigfoot...and ghosts and UFOs. You'd think everyone has gone mad."

Vito looked in his rearview mirror. He'd been doing it every ten seconds, waiting for the flatbed cap to come flying off and an enraged bigfoot to leap through the rear window. "I guess we know better now, don't we?"

Shay settled deep into the seat, an enormous, satisfied grin plastered all over his face. "That we do, buddy. That we do. And the whole world is going to know our names by the end of the week. Hey, where are we going?"

Vito took the exit a little faster than he'd intended. "To find a gas station and change out of these clothes. Maybe clean up a little."

"Guess I'm stinking. I didn't bring a change of clothes."

"Don't worry, I have enough in the back." Working for Parks and Rec, Vito was often in need of fresh shirts and pants. He was pretty sure there were extras for Shay in his bag.

They cruised into an Exxon station. Thankfully, the bathroom access was outside and they didn't need to ask for a key. If either of them had to enter the station's little mart, people would run from the place gagging. Shay went first while Vito pumped gas. He pulled the truck to the restroom area and waited for Shay to come out.

"Much better," Vito said when Shay emerged. "Just throw those clothes out."

Shay frowned. "But that's my favorite flannel shirt."

"Katie will stick her foot so far up your ass if you try to put that in your washer, she'll be able to tickle your nostrils with her toes."

"Fair point." Shay stuffed his soiled shirts and pants into a blue plastic barrel.

Vito had to hold his breath while he changed, the lingering stench Shay left in the bathroom a physical assault on his senses. He changed quickly and used up the bottle of hand soap on the sink to thoroughly scrub his hands, arms and face.

When he came out, Shay drew him into a hug and sniffed. "You smell like rose petals and honeydew."

Vito pushed him away as he laughed. "Get off of me, weirdo. You get too sentimental when you drink."

"We Irish are a sentimental folk. Whereas you meatballs are quite the pain in the ass when you've gone over your limit. Newsflash – nobody's looking at you."

"Idiot."

"Idiot lover. Now, I say we stop and get a proper drink before we go home."

That actually sounded like a great idea. Vito needed something a little stronger to take the edge off his nerves, but not too much so he couldn't drive them back to the Bronx. "Okay. But only for an hour. Then we have to hit the road and figure out what we're going to do with that thing."

Shay whooped and jumped into the truck, drumming his hands on the dash. Vito found a place called Bert's Bar in one of the smaller strip malls. There was a light crowd of what appeared to be regulars. Two televisions behind the bar were tuned to the Knicks game.

Vito and Shay settled onto a pair of stools at the far end of the bar. Shay ordered them each a glass of Jameson Black Barrel on the rocks. As always, Shay proposed a toast. He was the toastmaster general at every bar in their neighborhood.

"Vito, my friend, here's to a whole new world."

They tapped glasses. The whisky went down smooth and warm and was just what Vito needed. He went for a light beer next while Shay ordered another Jameson. Bert's was about as cozy as a bar could get, and an hour quickly turned into two. Luckily, their wives baked in an extra few hours for their return when they went hunting, knowing a quick stop in a pub would stretch on.

They'd better shove off and get back on the road. That bigfoot wasn't staying in Vito's truck all night.

"I gotta hit the head," Vito said. He could tell by the way Shay weaved on his barstool that he was feeling no pain.

"Remember. If you shake it more than twice, you're just playing with it."

Vito ordered a coffee before he headed off to the restroom. He was feeling much calmer now, but thoughts of what they were going to do with the body buzzed in his brain like a nest of murder hornets.

After making sure to only shake twice, he left the restroom to find another man in his seat next to Shay. As Vito got closer, he heard Shay say, "I'm not shitting you. A great big bigfoot! He was just lying there dead as a stump and we took him. Wait until you see it on the news. It'll blow your freaking mind."

Vito quickly got between them and reached for his coffee. "Did you tell him about the Loch Ness monster you caught off of Montauk Beach?"

Shay looked at him quizzically.

Vito turned to the stranger. "Guy's got more stories."

"I can tell," the older man said, winking. "I love a good fish story, but hunting stories are even better. And this is one I'd never heard before."

Shay tapped Vito on the back. "You can't get a Loch Ness monster in Long Island. They live in Scotland."

The man nodded at the coffee in Vito's hand. "Good luck with your friend. And bigfoot." He slipped away, headed for the restroom.

Whirling on Shay, Vito whispered, "What the hell is wrong with you?"

Shay's eye wobbled. "I think...I think I had too much to drink." He started to sag to the left.

"Really? I hadn't noticed. Luckily, that guy thinks it was all just drunk talk."

Leaning into him, Shay said, "Take me home, but promise you won't take advantage of me."

Vito couldn't be mad at Shay. He made him drink a cup of black coffee and they got back in the truck. This time, he drove under the speed limit, wanting to take some time so Shay could sober up enough to function on his own two feet.

They didn't make it home until a little after ten. The lights were off in both houses, but the porch lights blazed. Vito remembered Shay telling him that Katie had an early shift. Danielle was going to have dinner at her sister's two blocks away, which meant they were going to plow through bottles of wine and watch Hallmark Christmas movies. She was most likely asleep, while Meredith would be in her room with her ear buds in, watching stuff online.

"Home sweet home," Shay said, slurring much less than earlier. The man was a machine. He got out without so much as a bob or a weave. Keeping his voice low, he said, "We can't just leave him back there. What if someone steals him?"

"More like, what if someone smells him? Anyone walks past my truck, they'll call the cops swearing there's a dead body in there. And they'll be right."

Shay leaned against the truck. "We can't bring it into our houses."

"No, but how about your shed?"

Shay's little tin shed housed a lawnmower, a rake and some shovels. There was plenty of room for the bigfoot.

Taking a deep breath, and then scrunching up his face because they were too close to the back of the truck, he said, "Guess that's the best place for now. He only needs to be there until morning when we can get our ducks in a row."

"I'll get my wheelbarrow."

Vito opened the basement door and quietly brought out the wheelbarrow along with a heavy drop cloth. The bigfoot wouldn't exactly fit, but they could make it work. Theirs was a small block of houses with very little foot traffic. Shay kept a lookout, but a single soul wasn't out and about. That would change later when the bars closed and folks stumbled home.

It took some finagling to get the huge body into the wheelbarrow and at one point, Vito was pretty sure he'd aggravated his old sports hernia. Shay covered the body with the drop cloth. It took every bit of strength they had left to wheel the damn thing into the yard. Once it was in the shed, Shay snuck into his house, coming back with a plastic bag.

"What's in there?" Vito said softly.

"Car air fresheners. I bought a bunch for 75% off when that car wash on McLean went out of business. Help me open them."

They opened pack after pack of air fresheners, the mélange of fruit, pine and new car scents almost as gag-worthy as the bigfoot's natural musk. Once one was opened, it was tossed on the carcass. Covered in a couple of dozen cardboard trees, the bigfoot corpse was locked away.

"Let's meet in my yard at eight," Shay said. "We'll have to strategize."

Vito wondered how you strategized for showing the world that a monster really existed. Right now, he was too tired to even think about how to spell his name.

"Eight. Right."

There was a twinkle in Shay's eyes as he headed into his house, but not before getting naked and putting Vito's clothes in a black garbage bag. Vito did the same and hoped Meredith didn't wander out of her room when he crept into the house. He was surely permanently scarred from this night. He didn't need his daughter to be as well.

CHAPTER SIX

Shay Walsh fumbled about his house, exhaustion and too much whisky and beer taking their toll on him. He showered in the downstairs bathroom, wrapped a towel around his waist and did his best to avoid the creakiest parts of the stairs. His wife Katie was out like a light, thanks to the Ambien she'd taken to make sure she got a good eight hours of sleep in before her shift at the hospital.

With a heavy sigh, Shay got into a pair of boxers and old Westchester County Fair t-shirt, slipped under the covers and settled into the pillow.

He thought of their to-do list tomorrow. First, get the contact information for the major news outlets. Second, should they get a lawyer? No, first was telling the family what they had in the shed. Katie would have to call in to work. He'd need her here, with him and Caitlin. It was going to be a hurricane of a day. The first of many to come.

Despite the excitement lighting up his brain, he was soon snoring like a buzzsaw.

When Vito Esposito looked at himself in the mirror, he wondered who the person was staring back at him. For one of the rare times in his life, he was scared.

Scared that they'd brought a monster to their home.

Scared at the possibilities of all the things that could go wrong.

Scared at what this meant for society at large. How would proof of bigfoot affect people? Or for that matter, the wildlife that would certainly be disturbed as the curious turned out in droves looking for sasquatches.

Worried, not necessarily scared, at how quickly their lives could change. It couldn't all be riches and fame without some consequences.

He passed by his daughter's door and heard her singing along to some vaguely familiar pop song. His wife was curled on her side in bed. She didn't take note of his coming to bed. Vito tumbled into sleep, dragging his fear with him.

The creature's eyes fluttered open and it bolted upright, gasping. The wheelbarrow tilted over, depositing the bigfoot onto the floor. Its head clanged against the lawnmower. It was too disoriented to notice the buzzing spot of pain in its thick skull.

Remaining still, its broad chest panted rapidly as consciousness flooded its brain and body. Nothing felt right, looked right, and especially, smelled right. A riot of foreign odors assaulted its nose. With eyes adapted to see well in the dark, it found the source of the foul odors. Small things, smelly things, were on the ground around the beast. It flicked them away with a mighty paw, and then sniffed its fingers, recoiling at the stench.

Pushing itself up by its arms, it almost collapsed. Weakness had a cold grip on its muscles.

The bigfoot looked around the cramped space.

This was not home.

This was not a place it had ever seen before.

Unfamiliarity made the hair on its back rise.

It opened all its senses, searching for predator or prey.

It wanted to get out, to be free from this place-like-no-place. From these scents that were interfering with its ability to properly smell.

When it stood, its head once again came in contact with something hard. The shed's ceiling dented outward. The bigfoot hunched its shoulders. It reached out to the vertical seam that allowed a sliver of light through. Its fingers grazed a texture that was very new. It was cold as the stream but smooth, like a summer leaf.

The bigfoot jammed its fingers into the seam as if tunneling out of a deep hole toward the sun. A screeching sound made the bigfoot stop, pull away. The noise stopped as well.

Leaning forward and tentatively sniffing the air coming through the opening, it was confused even more. What were these things it sensed on the night winds? As much as it didn't like what it was detecting, it was better than the inside of this place-like-no-place. Confined spaces were not something the bigfoot encountered in the wild. It felt trapped, in danger.

It made a fist and punched one of the doors off the track. The door folded in on itself and skittered across the lawn.

The cold night air was a welcome relief from the cloying confines of the place-like-no-place. What wasn't a relief was the creature's surroundings. There were no trees, just strange, large structures everywhere. It stood on grass, the small patch that it was, but it gave way to rock. So much rocky surface, yet level. The bigfoot remained impossibly still as it would in its home if something came too close. It listened for the approach of an intruder. What it heard was muted voices, its heightened sense of hearing caught in a whirlwind of noise emanating from the boxy places.

Where was this place and how had it gotten here?

The creature remembered chasing the deer. The cold time was fast approaching and like all mammals, the bigfoot needed to eat as much as it could, while it could. It had sensed other things around the field, the beings that it had long ago learned to stay away from. But its hunger ran riot over the need to stay hidden. The kill had been an easy one. The hot meat had sent a thrill of electricity through the bigfoot's body.

Then there had been a sharp pain, and emptiness.

It had to get out of here.

It ran across the lawn and onto the cold hard surface that gave it pause. Was this a safe thing to walk upon? It tested the yield, making sure it wouldn't break. Good. It didn't feel right beneath its feet, but at least it wasn't sending it tumbling to its doom.

The bigfoot walked down the alley and into the street where more strange objects were lined up on both sides of the path. The moonlight reflected off their surface. At first, the bigfoot stopped and jumped back into the shadows, wary that these things might be alive. It watched them for several minutes, again still as a statue, and when there was no detectable life, it crept forward.

Perhaps they were some kind of natural wall or barrier. No matter, the bigfoot would give them a wide berth.

Lights blazed overhead and more lights and sounds came from the boxes all around it.

The sensory overload was too much. The bigfoot bumped into something inconsequential to it and ran. The garbage can went flying, discarding plastic bags of trash that broke open on impact with the ground.

Away. It must get away.

As the bigfoot ran down the street, something that looked like the things on the path sped by just ahead of it with terrifying speed. It also blazed with light and sound. What kinds of horrible creatures populated this strange world?

The darkness beckoned, and just past the spot where the light and noisy, shiny thing ran by was a wall, and beyond it, pitch black. There were trees as well, and stones, so many stones jutting from the soil and grass.

Making sure no other moving things were about, the bigfoot sprinted to the wall and leaped over the iron railing. It landed on the other side with a resounding thud and continued running deep into the night, negotiating its way around the stones. It ran past pools of water and under swaying trees, the scent of earth and almost-home settling its racing heart.

It stopped before what looked like the entrance to a cave, though this one had a strange, covered opening. Flowers had been placed by the cave.

A pair of moving lights moved about in the distance, along with the sound of gravel crunching. The twin lights appeared to be coming this way. The bigfoot knew much about caves, even though this one had a barrier like the place it had awoken within earlier. And just like the other, the bigfoot used its strength and fear to bash its way through. This space was cold but not as cramped as the other. The bigfoot dipped inside and away from the lights.

It settled into a corner and, weariness suddenly taking over, slumped slowly to the ground. The cooing of an owl was the last thing it heard before it slipped back into the darkness.

And the Woodlawn Cemetery lay still in the night as it had for over a century.

CHAPTER SEVEN

Shay should have been hungover and unable to lift his pounding head off the pillow. Excitement (and his stealthy Irish genes) had him up before the alarm he'd set and practically giddy. Katie was still out, her arm over her head as she snored.

He peed, brushed his teeth and put on some clothes, all while humming a nonsense tune that was merely an expression of his happiness. Lord knows, the Walsh house needed some happiness.

Caitlin was still asleep, buried under a mountain of blankets.

Shay guzzled a bottle of water while the coffee percolated on the stove. They had one of those single cup coffee makers, a gift from Katie's mother, but those K cups were expensive and the coffee never tasted as good as it did coming from the old pot they'd bought at a tag sale when they'd moved into this house.

Sun peeked through the kitchen blinds. Shay fired up his laptop, ready to do some intense researching once Vito was up. He made sure his phone was charged. A lot of calls were going to be made today.

Pouring himself a cup of hot coffee and his humming having turned to whistling, Shay opened the blinds to the window that overlooked the yard where the shed and his miracle find awaited.

The coffee mug slipped from his fingers and clattered into the sink. He didn't even feel the hot coffee as is splashed on his arms and hands.

"What in the blue fuck?"

One of the shed doors was in a mangled heap, lying in the grass like a used tissue. The other door that had somehow stayed on the track had been bent nearly in half.

He could see right into the shed.

The wheelbarrow was tipped over on the floor. The tree air fresheners were scattered about.

And the bigfoot was gone!

"Jesus, Jesus, Jesus."

Shay sprinted the three houses down to Vito's in his bare feet and resisted pounding on the front door. Instead, he ran to the backyard and tossed a pebble against Vito's bedroom window. "Vito," he called up, trying not to shout.

Two more pebbles later, the window flew open and Vito stuck his head out. "Christ, Shay. What is wrong with you?"

Vito looked like he'd barely slept. Dark stubble dotted his head.

"It's gone," Shay said, hopping from foot to foot.

Vito stared at him a moment, until dark clarity clouded his face. "What do you mean it's gone?"

The hinges of Shay's jaw pulsed with dull agony. "You should see my shed. It must have woken up and busted the whole thing open."

Ducking his head inside for a moment, Vito came back out and hissed, "Stay right there."

Less than a minute later, Vito was standing beside Shay, dressed in a robe and slippers. "I thought you said that thing was dead." His eyes darted around the yard as if he were expecting the escaped bigfoot to come vaulting over the fence. "And keep your voice down. Danielle is still sleeping."

"I thought it was dead. Did *you* see it breathe?"

"No. But it was hard to tell under all that hair. Christ, what are we gonna do?"

Shay's heart felt like it was going to explode from his chest. He needed a good, stiff drink in the worst way. "How the hell should I know? It's probably already caught. I mean, it's not exactly like it's going to blend into the environment."

"Did you check the news?" Vito paced around his patio set.

"No. As soon as I saw it was gone, I came straight here."

Vito patted his robe pockets. "Shit. My phone's upstairs."

"Come to my house. We'll check there."

The two men stalked to Shay's, smiling and waving when Mrs. Adeline across the street, the grand matron and queen gossip of the neighborhood, spotted them from her perch in the front window and nodded.

Shay turned on the little television on the kitchen counter and punched in the channel for the local news. A story about the Girl Scouts painting signs for Bronx businesses rolled on. They checked the crawl under the video. Nothing about a bigfoot running around the streets of New York.

Shay offered Vito coffee, which he declined. They watched in silence for fifteen minutes, until the news cycle repeated itself.

"It has to still be out there," Shay said.

"Or it just hasn't hit the news. That's the kind of thing the cops might want to keep under wraps for a little while."

Shay bit his bottom lip. "No way. There would be witnesses. Animal control, maybe. Cops, definitely. We'd hear about it."

"Coming from the man who thought the bigfoot was dead and convinced me it would be a good idea to cart its smelly ass home." Vito slumped into a chair and drank his coffee.

"It's still out there. It has to be at least hurt. It can't have gotten far. We need to find it."

"Oh sure. I'll borrow Meredith's old butterfly net. No problem."

Shay leaned against the refrigerator and gave a dramatic sigh. "It is our problem. If it hurts anyone, it's on us." He thought about what it had done to that buck and shivered. Would it see a family dog as food? Or the family itself? "We have to find it."

"And do what? Shoot it? We try walking around here with a gun and we'll be in the Tombs by lunch."

"There has to be some way. And if we find it before someone else, we'll get right back on track." Shay went to the window and looked at his ruined shed. He wasn't surprised none of them had heard it last night. Katie was drugged, he was drunk and he'd bet his last nickel Meredith had slept with her ear buds in. And it wasn't as if they slept in some bucolic rural outpost. Noises at night were expected, as long as it didn't involve gunfire, which rarely happened in their neck of the Bronx.

Snapping his fingers, Shay pointed at Vito and said, "We can trap it!"

Vito raised an eyebrow. "Trap it? How? Bro, this isn't a game. You saw what that thing can do. If we get too close, it'll use our arms as drumsticks and pound our heads like it was John Bonham."

"I haven't gotten to that part yet. Yeah, we'll find a way to trap it."

Vito finished his coffee. "You're forgetting one thing."

"What's that?"

"We have to find it first."

Shay lifted the window. The smell of fall leaves and a faint odor of musk floated into the kitchen. "That's the easy part. We just follow that smell."

"What smell?"

Caitlin startled them as she stood in the kitchen entrance wearing a My Chemical Romance tee and fluffy bunny pajama bottoms Katie had found at Five Below. Her phone was glued to her hand as usual and her hair looked like it had been teased for a metal video in 1987.

Shay did his best to hide his surprise. "Oh, hey pumpkin. Your uncle and I were just talking about how you find fall carnivals. You...you just follow the smell of sausage and pepper and fried dough."

It was a supremely dumb thing to say, but it was the best he could come up with. He hadn't been to or seen a fall carnival in this neck of the not-woods since well before Caitlin was born.

Vito patted his stomach. "Nothing better than a carnival zeppole."

She looked from one to the other and said, "Weird. We have any Cinnamon Toast Crunch left?"

By the time Shay poured a bowl for his daughter, her ear buds were back in and she was fixated on her phone's screen. Before she left to go back to her room, she pulled one out and said, "What time are we going trick or treating?"

Shay wanted to slap his forehead. That's right. It was Halloween. He'd totally forgotten. There wouldn't be many more trick or treating years left for Caitlin.

"I figure around five, right when it's getting dark. Sound good?"

She eyed him, searching his soul for…for what?

She knows something's off. Quick, distract her!

"And after, you can pick out any horror movie you want and we'll all watch it together."

"Seriously? Any movie?"

Mission accomplished. Though he was sure he was going to regret this.

"It's Halloween. Anything goes."

"Sweet."

She turned and went up to her room, spooning sugar that masqueraded as cereal into her mouth.

"Katie's gonna kill you."

It was true. She held the reins when it came to raising a sane daughter in an insane world. Shay knew Caitlin was going to pick some R rated disaster. His only hope of not heading for the dog house was to distract his wife with the big news he and Vito had found a bigfoot and they were all about to get rich.

Shay closed his eyes and shook his head. He could see the odds of a happy ending spiraling away from him.

"Right," he said. "Let's think of a way to keep the big bad bigfoot down and get to sniffing. We only have to find it, trap it, and get the full credit before five o'clock."

Vito scratched at the kitchen table. "We are so fucked."

CHAPTER EIGHT

Maura Faherty knew she should be crying. She was flanked by her weeping daughter and son, both of them holding onto her for dear life.

What is wrong with me?

True, she'd never been the most emotional person on the planet. Quite a few times during arguments with her husband, Michael would call her an ice bitch, thinking it would cut her down. In actuality, it propped her up – a statement of fact that meant nothing he said could pierce her too deeply.

But that was only a part of their story. She'd loved Michael and appreciated all he did for them. Maybe she didn't say it or show it as much as she should have, but he knew.

Right?

If there was ever a time to let the water works flow, standing beside your husband's coffin in a cold cemetery was it.

So why was she just gawking at the cave like a mannequin? The angrier she got with herself, the deeper her sorrow burrowed to the recesses of her mind.

What will people think if I don't shed a single tear? They'll whisper later that I'm glad he's gone. The cancer was no picnic, but at least the ice bitch no longer has to fake being the happy wife. They don't know me! Michael was the outgoing one. They have no clue about our relationship!

Father Adebayo, a recent transplant to the parish from Nigeria, went through all the proper motions. Maura didn't pay attention. Dozens of people from Michael's life stood behind her and the children. She heard their sniffles or outright sobbing. Even Drew, Michael's burly friend from the processing plant, had huge crocodile tears cascading down his cheeks.

That's the problem. They don't know me because I never let them in. But they'll think they have me all summed up now.

Jesus, Michael, why did you have to leave us? Had I been enough for you? You never complained. Well, at least not when we weren't in a tiff. I can't face these people alone. I can't do what they expect me to do. I don't know why. I'm a little broken, but you knew that about me.

Donnie and Bernadette clutched her hands. She'd said she was going to be strong for them, but was this too strong? What would they think? That's what she cared about more than anything else. She was lessening herself in their eyes, and it hurt.

Lean into it. Let it swallow you whole.

Father Adebayo paused and looked to Maura. She had no idea what he was expecting from her because she hadn't followed a word he'd said. She wished she'd brought her dark sunglasses so he couldn't see the confusion in her eyes. He gave a gentle nod, as if to say, *I understand, you've been through so much and this all is overwhelming.* He was correct, just not in the way she assumed he thought.

The priest gestured toward Roy Flynn and his kilted bagpipers. Flynn had been a bar buddy of Michael's and had offered the bagpiper's services at the funeral. Michael had loved the bagpipes. She thought they were shrill and irritating. There was no way she could say no. Besides, she wanted to give her husband a good, proper Irish burial. She hoped Michael was somewhere close so he could hear them play for him.

Gerald Cacek stepped forward and rapped on the huge bass drum strapped to the front of his chest while Paddy Fitzsimmons went to work on his snare drum. Seconds later, the bagpipes joined in. Maura squeezed her children's hands and felt a tear coming on.

The bigfoot went from a dead sleep to on its feet and fully awake in the blink of an eye.

Something was pounding in the distance. A deep thudding mixed with some kind of animal wailing. It was like no forest creature the bigfoot had ever heard before.

The wailing got louder, more insistent. It pierced through the bigfoot's head like a sword fresh from the forge.

It made the creature woozy, like the times it ate certain berries and mushrooms that always made it sick but there had been some pleasure before it got worse.

The high-pitched screeching escalated. The pounding boom-boom-boomed in the bigfoot's marrow.

It was too much to bear.

The beast emerged from the crypt with its hands over its ears.

Rage.

That's what this noise was birthing within the animal's breast.

This caterwauling had to be stopped.

The bigfoot squinted against the harsh daylight, zeroed in on the source of the head-splitting sound and ran.

Maura nearly exalted with relief when she felt the first wet tear slide down her face. It was as much a finger in the eye of anyone who was thinking bad thoughts of her as it was an affirmation that she wasn't completely dead inside. A smile escaped from her tight control. The priest noticed the smile and made a face that worried her.

Oh dear. What have I done? You can't smile at your husband's funeral!

She bent her head to look at her children as much as to hide her face. Bernadette's little shoulders shook with sobs. Donnie took a shuddering breath while he stared at his father's coffin.

The bagpipers eased into Amazing Grace.

Keeping her eyes on the tops of her children's heads, Maura didn't see what started the obliteration of Michael's funeral service. But she did feel a displacement of the air above her, as if something large and heavy had flown just over her head.

Maura looked up and into the round, terrified eyes of Father Adebayo.

The bagpipers in the front still played, the overall swell of Amazing Grace diminishing quickly as the ones at the back dropped their instruments and ran in every which direction. Sean Mulligan hopped over a tombstone, his kilt bouncing up toward his midriff. At that moment, Maura confirmed that the bagpipers indeed wore nothing underneath their kilts.

People started screaming behind her.

At first, Maura was confused. What was happening? What sick person was breaking up her husband's funeral?

And then Gerald Cacek turned to look behind him. A huge, hairy fist punched through his bass drum. Another one cold-cocked Gerald so hard, his head spun all the way around – twice! He crumpled to the ground and the music stopped.

"What in the name of sweet Jesus!" Roy Flaherty exclaimed a split-second before the seven foot tall hairy creature kicked him in the balls. Even though Maura was ten feet away from Roy, she could hear something rupture in his groin. His eyes went to the top of his head and he uttered a strained, "Oof!" while clutching his crotch and falling onto his side. He rolled until he came to rest beside Michael's coffin.

The mourners scattered. Hands tugged and clutched at Maura, but her legs wouldn't move. The children yelped and cowered behind her.

"No! Noooo!" Father Adebayo stutter-stepped backward, his hands up, the Bible slipping from his fingers. The creature grabbed hold of another bagpiper and tossed him into a tree. Leaves rained down around them.

Maura should have picked up the children and run for her life, but she couldn't snap out of her paralysis.

The monster grabbed a bagpipe from the ground and it made a windy, dying sound. That seemed to enrage the creature even more. It lashed out and snagged Dermot Feeny's collar. Dermot shrieked like a banshee and tried to bat the paw away. The monster drew the bagpipe back and stabbed it into the poor man's rectum. What came out of Dermot's mouth would forever haunt Maura's dreams. It was a solo of agony unlike any she could have ever imagined.

The beast flicked Dermot aside, but with enough power to send the coffin crashing into the open grave where it landed on its side.

To Maura's horror, the lid popped open and Michael's body appeared to jump almost out of it on his own.

Sweet Mary in heaven!

The force of the impact split the stitching on Michael's eyes and mouth, all three opening and revealing death in its truest form.

Before Maura passed out, she saw Father Adebayo rushing toward her, his white vestment billowing out like a parachute as he wrapped her and Donnie and Bernadette in his holy embrace.

The creature jumped over the open grave and ran past them, away from the direction of the fleeing mourners and bagpipers. It slipped out of sight behind a mausoleum as Maura fell into darkness.

Just before she lost consciousness, she thought, *Thank God I cried.*

CHAPTER NINE

Shay ushered Vito out of the house when he heard Katie up and about upstairs.

"I'll meet you in my yard in fifteen minutes, yeah?" Shay said as he pushed Vito out the back door.

"I have to get dressed anyway. What are you going to tell Katie?"

Shay gripped the edge of the door. "You think the truth will work?"

Vito rubbed his eyes until they were red. "I don't think Katie or Danielle will believe it."

"That's because they're not crazy."

He shut the door, poured a cup of coffee for Katie and went upstairs. His hand was so unsteady, he spilled droplets of coffee all over the stairs and hall. His wife was coming out of the bathroom just as he entered the bedroom.

"Look at you up bright and early," she said, tying her hair up. She took off her night shirt and shorts and went to the closet to get her uniform. She looked as young and beautiful as the day they'd said their vows at St. Barnabas Church. Shay knew he was a lucky man, but never more so than when she was just like this. "I thought you'd be down for the count today. I assume you stopped at a bar to drink your sorrows away." She gave him a smile that said she was only having some fun with him. He offered her the coffee. "Wow, exceeding all expectations today. Does this mean you did catch a deer?"

Shay sat on the corner of the bed. "Is there any chance you can call out today?"

Katie slipped into her white slacks. "Why? Is something wrong? Where's Caitlin?"

She was on instant high alert, already thinking of worst case scenarios. It was in her nature, which was what made her an excellent ER nurse.

"Caitlin's fine and before you ask, nobody died."

Her shoulders sagged. "Okay. Good. So why do you want me to take the day off? I'm not cleaning the deer. That's yours and Vito's job."

"We didn't get a deer."

She hesitated putting on her shirt, the one with the pink and purple butterflies. "So what is it then? I can't just call out. I have to find someone to cover for me, you know."

What was implied there, whether she meant it or not, was that they needed the money her shift would bring, so this better be good.

"I know this is going to sound ambiguous and strange, but Vito and I need to take care of something today and I can't bring Caitlin along with us. I promise, we'll be done before trick or treating." At least he hoped.

Katie's brows knit and she gave him a long and silent stare, waiting for him to crack. He withered like an ant under a magnifying glass amplifying the sun.

Willing himself not to stammer, he said, "It's a surprise."

"A surprise."

He scratched the back of his neck. "Yeah, a Halloween surprise."

"And it's so big, I need to stay home?" Katie looked like she wasn't buying what he was selling.

"I just need you to trust me on this one."

"That's what people say before things get bad in a hurry," Katie said.

"I find your lack of faith in me troubling." He gave her his best smile, hoping to melt the iceberg of her distrust.

She stared at him for a long while, willing him to crack, and then sighed. "Fine. I'll see if Chyree can cover for me."

He put her face in his hands and kissed her. "You're the best, babe."

"All I know is, this better be good."

Shay hoped it would be, too.

Vito found Danielle and Meredith in the kitchen making breakfast. Danielle was frying up some bacon while Meredith got the butter and milk out of the refrigerator. The house smelled wonderful. Frying bacon always got his appetite revving.

"Hey baby," Danielle said. "I'm sorry I wasn't up when you came home last night. My sister wined and dined me pretty good."

"Hi daddy," Meredith chirped. "Mom and Aunt Jennifer were drunk."

Vito kissed Danielle on the lips and Meredith on the top of her head. "You don't say."

"Meredith!" Danielle snapped, but there was no venom in it. "No bacon for you."

"They spent all night laughing like crazy, and then they cried like babies," Meredith said. She rolled her eyes and Vito laughed. He didn't think it was possible to laugh with this much tension coiling his insides up.

"It was a sad movie," Danielle said.

"It was a boring movie."

"You'll feel different when you're my age, kiddo." Danielle took Vito in and said, "Where were you in your robe and slippers? Did you and Shay finally get a deer? Please tell me it's at Shay's house. I don't want a dead animal in our yard."

Vito wasn't prepared to tell Danielle the story, not now and especially not with Meredith in the room. "Uh, I heard something knock the garbage cans down. Must have been that stray cat that's been poking around lately."

"I left it a can of cat food the other night," Meredith said.

Danielle pointed the spatula at her. "I told you not to feed it."

"But it's all alone and hungry."

"That thing is almost as big as a dog. I don't think hunger is one of its problems."

Meredith looked like she was about to cry. Vito reached across the table and took her hand. "I think that was very nice of you. Where did you find cat food?"

"I bought it at the corner store with my own money."

"How about this. I'll buy a bunch of cans so you can feed it every night. Sound good?"

Her eyes lit up.

Danielle piped in, "As long as it stays an outdoor cat. I don't want this to be the gateway to having that puma in the house."

Vito was about to reassure her when the phone rang. They were one of the last families around to have a landline because Danielle's mother refused to learn a new number, so calling their cell phones was out. Stubborn as a mule, that woman was.

Meredith popped out of her seat like bread from a toaster and grabbed the phone.

"Oh, hi Uncle Shay. Yes, he's here." She held the phone out to Vito. "It's for you."

Vito's stomach dropped. All thoughts of having bacon and toast went right out the window. "What's up?"

"I told her."

Vito shot a secret look at Danielle to see if she was listening in. She was too busy concentrating on the bacon. She was a great cook and even something as simple as bacon required her to pour all of her time and attention so every strip came out perfect.

"How'd it go?" Vito asked, expecting Shay to warn him that Katie was coming over to tell Danielle their husbands must have really tied one on last night and now were covering up what they did with a ridiculous story.

"Are you crazy? Of course I didn't tell her we stole a bigfoot. You ready to go hunting?"

Vito got up and went into the living room, stretching the cord as far as it would go. He lowered his voice and said, "Easier said than done. We don't even know where it is."

"I have an idea of where it could have gone. Get your rifle but keep it in the bag. We have a sasquatch to catch."

CHAPTER TEN

The bigfoot ran throughout Woodlawn Cemetery tirelessly, desperate to find a place to hide. There were plenty of rocks sticking out of the ground everywhere, but nothing large enough to disappear behind for a while.

Its steps faltered as hunger took over. It stumbled to a small pond, leaping over the hard ground it didn't like to get to the grass. Cautiously getting down on all fours, it drank greedily. The water was cold and had a strange tinge that would have caused the bigfoot to pull away if not for the roaring thirst that had its stomach grumbling.

What did stop it from slaking its thirst was the sound of distant wailing, like the chorus of dozens of deranged birds. The police sirens frightened the bigfoot and sent it back into motion. It ran, jumping over tombstones and ducking under low branches. Up ahead there was another tall fence, and beyond that, the shiny things that moved so quickly up and down the strange path. There were more of them than ever in the light of day.

The creature did not like the shiny things. They moved too fast. Faster than it could hope to run, which meant they were a threat.

Cowering behind a tombstone, the bigfoot watched the shiny things come and go. The hair on its back rose as it heard the wild screeching come ever closer.

This was not a good place to hide. Not at all.

It had to get out. On the other side of the shiny things on the path was a patch of inviting woods. It didn't see any stones littering the ground between the trees.

It would go there.

Within the trees was some degree of darkness and most of all, safety.

Waiting until there was a moment where there were less shiny things on the path, the bigfoot sprinted, jumped, grabbed the top of the fence and pulled its massive bulk over, dropping onto the cold, unyielding sidewalk.

Head swiveling left and right, the beast darted into the road. A car driven by a mother with her two children in the back seat saw the blur of bulk and fur and stomped on the brakes as she mashed the heel of her hand onto the horn. The car fishtailed for a moment and the bigfoot turned to glare at the source of the noise. The mother locked eyes with the creature and went rigid, an atavistic fear pouring concrete into her arms and legs. Her heart danced erratically.

"What's that, mommy?" her six-year old daughter asked, straining against her seatbelt to get a better look at the fleeing bigfoot.

The woman couldn't bring herself to answer, because it was the same question she was asking herself.

She'd also peed, the spreading warmth of her seat bringing no sense of shame.

Later, she would tell herself it was just some idiot kid in a costume. But she would always wonder why that scant glimpse would cause such a physical reaction, or better yet, repulsion.

Even sleeping pills would fail to put an end to her restless nights.

Shay met Vito outside, both of their rifle bags slung over their shoulders.

The first thing they heard was the commotion coming from the cemetery across the street. The wail and blare of sirens from police, fire and rescue shattered the normal morning routine.

They also heard the squeal of tires and bleating of a horn from what sounded like just a few blocks away.

Vito turned to Shay. "You think that could be a coincidence?"

Shay sucked on his teeth for a bit and said, "No such thing. It makes sense going to the cemetery since its right across the street and sort of looks like the woods. Sounds like our monster got itself in some trouble."

They jogged to the end of their block and looked up East 233rd Street with the cemetery to their left. Not too far up ahead, a pair of brake lights turned off and a car slowly eased down the road.

On the right up that way was the entrance to Indian Field with its baseball fields, tennis and bocce courts. And beyond that was the woodsy extension of Van Cortlandt Park that went on for a small bit before coming to the soccer fields where Caitlin and Meredith played. Just beyond that, the park came to an end with a bus stop and the start of the neighboring city of Yonkers.

"You think it might still be in the cemetery?" Vito said. "Because we're in deep shit if we go in there toting rifles with cops around. We don't even know if they're in there because of the bigfoot."

His pulse racing, Shay said, "Oh, I'm sure that's why they're in there. That's not the sound of a cop funeral."

As if to confirm his feelings, a pair of ambulances tore past them, heading for the cemetery entrance, he was sure of it, around the corner. He raised an eyebrow at Vito.

"Fine. So now what do you suggest?"

"We have two areas where there's inviting greenery. If it left the cemetery, odds are it'll wind up in the woods in Van Cortlandt Park. If we're lucky…"

"Which we're not."

"It could have dipped into Indian Field. A lot less ground to cover. And cop-free."

"Well, then I'm taking the truck. It's only a few blocks, but the less time we're walking the streets with our guns, the better."

Shay didn't argue with him. He waited until Vito backed down the one-way street and climbed aboard. They hit the lone red light before the turn onto Van Cortlandt Park East. Shay's leg bounced as if he'd just downed ten energy drinks. He clung to the hope that they could nab the bigfoot and a bit of history.

Or, at the very least, they could be the heroes who stopped a rampaging bigfoot (if, in fact, it had done any rampaging). There had to be something good to come of that, right?

As long as we never tell a soul we're the fucking morons who brought it here, he thought as Vito made the turn and pulled into an open spot across the street from the park.

"Come up with a trap idea yet?" Vito asked. Shay couldn't tell if he was being sarcastic.

Shay had to admit, a trap was probably not a possibility. What kind of trap would they build, and where would they put it? Even something as simple as digging a hole and covering it with branches would take too much time and more than likely snag an innocent person, not a bigfoot.

He could see Indian Field and confirmed it was quite empty. No, the animal, man, monster, or whatever it was, would be hiding in the trees, not looking for a pickup baseball game.

There was a narrow, meandering path in there that his father used to take him on what he called Adventure Hikes. Shay remembered thinking they had entered a completely different world once they were enveloped by the trees and brush. It was a place where anything was possible. His young mind saw mighty snakes, heard the roar of tigers and the stomping of elephants.

They did find some arrowheads that Shay still had in a box on his dresser. As he got older, those same woods were more for bringing girls or having a few Budweiser nips than seeking adventure.

Well, you're finally getting a true blue adventure in the park.

Vito and Shay jogged across the street, stopping at a wood and concrete bench. An elderly man sat there, tossing crumbs of bread to a smattering of pigeons cooing around his feet.

"You see anything…strange go back there?" Shay asked.

The pigeons fluttered away.

The man squinted at them, then their rifle bags, and said, "No. I'd say you're the strangest things I've seen so far. But the day is young. And you scared my pigeons."

"If you do see something, you should probably run," Vito said, eyeing the woods behind the man.

"Are you kidding me? It'll take me five minutes just to get off this damn bench."

Shay nodded his head at the trees. "Come on. He'll be fine."

Vito hesitated. "You don't know that."

"What do you want me to do?"

The old man raised his hand. "I'm right here. What are you two bozos talking about?"

Shay was tempted to tell him, but bit his tongue. "It's probably best if you get a head start on going home."

"What if I don't? Are you gonna shoot me?"

Vito looked aghast. "What? No! Why would you say that?"

"Says the man carrying a rifle or a shotgun or whatever you have in there. If I had one of those cellphones, I'd call the cops."

Shay didn't need this. "They're not what you think. These are paintball guns. We're just going to test them out a little."

The man shook his head, his eyes downcast. "That's the stupidest thing I ever heard. Aren't you a little too old to be messing around with paint guns?"

Shay patted him on his bony shoulder. "It keeps us young."

As they walked around the bench, the man said, "That's what I have my blue pills for."

Walking into the trees, Vito said, "That's us in the future, you know."

Shay sniffed the air. They'd smell the bigfoot well before they saw it. He prayed it was still loopy from the tranquilizer and not at full strength and scared or angry. "If we make it that far."

Slowing their pace, they unzipped the bags and took their rifles out.

"Don't shoot until you absolutely see it," Vito warned. "There could be kids out here, or even joggers or people out for a little nature walk when we get to the path area."

"Really? Don't shoot kids? There goes my whole plan."

"Your whole plan is the reason we're out here. So cram your sarcasm up your ass."

They walked slowly, trying to avoid making noise, but it was impossible with all the leaf cover.

Taking in a deep breath, Shay said, "You're right. I'm an asshole. I'm just a little keyed up at the moment."

"Which is why I said to be careful. We don't want to have an accident we can't live with."

Rifles pointed at the ground, they probed deeper into the woods. Not that they went very deep here. They could hear cars whizzing by on the Major Deegan Expressway at the other end of the park. There was a chance the strange sound would preoccupy the bigfoot and it would miss their approach.

If it was here. The air smelled too clean. But there was more ground to cover.

Vito suddenly stopped. "I just thought of something."

"What's that?"

A squirrel chattered angrily at them from a branch above their heads.

"What if it goes to the playground?"

Shay's heart sank to somewhere near his ankles. "If it does, I guess we have to shoot to kill." Hadn't he seen in one of those documentaries on bigfoot that some of them were attracted to the sounds of children. That had always struck him as strange. What he assumed was that maybe they had the minds of children, and therefore, like is drawn to like.

Today being a Sunday and Halloween, there was sure to be a lot of people in the park.

"I don't think we're qualified to shoot at a bigfoot that big when it's surrounded by kids and their parents."

Knowing neither was exactly a dead-eye, they continued their search, each offering up a slew of Hail Marys. They needed all the help they could get.

CHAPTER ELEVEN

Something familiar tickled the creature's nose. It was not a scent of home. More like the residue of when it had been in the cramped place.

Hunkering behind a fallen log, the sasquatch waited, puzzling out what it could be or mean. Everything in its world related to survival. A smell could mean danger, or food, demark a specific location, or act as a beacon toward home.

It couldn't establish what this smell was.

Trying its best to blend into the environment while it waited for more information to dictate its next move, a series of shrieks came from its left. These were not the shrieks of the animals it shared its home with. And it certainly wasn't the unbearable sound of the things that drove it from its hiding place in the great field with all the stones.

They did not sound like a warning, or cries of fear.

They were almost…pleasant.

More came from that direction, piquing the bigfoot's interest. It no longer cared about the scent that befuddled its brain. The continued shrieking drew it out of its safe spot behind the log.

It had heard this sound once before, a long time ago. The image of the things that had made that noise flashed behind the bigfoot's eyes. It had liked watching those things and listening to them. At least at first.

Needing to see, it wended its way around the trees, the sounds pulling it like a magnet, growing louder with each and every step.

Gwendolyn Healy was determined not to be found by her friend Haley. In the world of hide and seek, Gwen was the best of all her friends and she was determined to keep it that way.

Hiding in the park wasn't easy, especially when her mother told her she absolutely, under no circumstances, could step even one foot outside the fence. There were trees on three sides of the park with plenty of great places to hide. It was tempting, but being taken from the park early and punished when she got home was enough to keep her within the gated confines of Woodlawn Playground.

All of the little kids were running around the teeter-totter and slides. Little was a big distinction for Gwen who was all of six-years old. The basketball courts were free from the big kids and men who would fill them later in the day, but there wasn't any cover there. The swings section wasn't much better.

Sure, there were a couple of skinny trees (where Dina and Mary hid and were quickly found) and the little house where the men who cleaned the park kept their things. That wouldn't do for Gwen Healy, world champion lost and founder!

A pair of moms sat side by side on one of the park benches by the back of the park, their oversized strollers in front of them. Gwen had snuck behind that bench and crawled under it, well hidden by the strollers and four jean-clad legs.

Seeing Haley walking in circles calling out for her nearly made her giggle and give herself away. Pretty soon, Haley would quit and Gwen would win…again.

Waiting under the bench, she thought about her Princess Elsa costume and how much she couldn't wait to go trick or treating later. She hoped she got a lot of gummy worms. She loved gummy worms more than anything. Oh, and Snickers bars.

Her visions of Halloween were interrupted by a very bad smell. One of the mothers shifted in her seat and said, "Oh! Did the sewer back up?"

The other said, "More like something died in the woods. Maybe the wind shifted."

Gwen had to pinch her nose. Her small mind couldn't come up with any words to label what she was smelling. *Very, very bad* summed it up quite nicely.

Squirming under the bench, she turned to face the woods. Yes, it was definitely coming from there. The stench practically slapped her in the face.

"I can't stay here," one of the mothers said.

"Me neither. Wow, that's nasty. Smells like someone set a pile of old dog crap on fire."

The woman's eyebrows arched. "Is that a smell you're familiar with?"

The other woman rolled her eyes. "Let's just get upwind of this, okay?"

They hustled away, one trying to extract just how the other knew what burning dog shit smelled like.

Suddenly, Gwen's hiding spot was utterly exposed. Luckily, Haley was at the other end of the park, poking around the slides.

Gwen was about to dash for another place to hide when she saw something in the woods that stopped her cold.

Why was a man in a big gorilla suit standing on the other side of the fence? And most of all, why did his costume smell like that?

Unlike her little brother, Gwen wasn't afraid of costumes. She begged her mother to take her to the Stew Leonard's supermarket every weekend on the off chance she could high five the cow or chicken.

Extracting herself from her place beneath the bench, Gwen said, "Happy Halloween."

The man in the gorilla suit, who had been watching the kids playing, looked at her. The mask was so real, she almost thought she was at the zoo in the Congo Gorilla Forest enclosure.

"I like your costume," she said. Her small thumb and forefinger still had her nose pinched closed. "But it really stinks. Peeyeew." She fanned her hand across her face for emphasis.

The man stepped fully out of the trees and through the break in the fence. He was hunched over as if he were ready to duck at any time. He seemed to have forgotten all about the other kids. This made Gwen a little nervous. She wasn't supposed to talk to strangers. Even on Halloween. Then again, he wasn't talking, so maybe this was okay.

Some baby started crying and the man squatted down until most of him was hidden behind the row of benches.

"Got you!"

Gwen whirled around and faced a triumphant Haley. Her pigtails were festooned with little plastic ghosts her mom had bought for her. Dina and Mary were right behind her.

"No fair," Gwen said. "He made me stop hiding."

"Who?"

Gwen pointed to the cowering man in the gorilla costume.

"Eeeewwwww," Mary groaned. Haley and Dina's faces screwed up once the smell wafted their way.

"Why is he hiding?" Haley asked. "Did he do something bad?"

"I don't know," Gwen said, shrugging her shoulders. "But it's the best costume ever."

With her hands on her hips, Haley addressed the man, "And why won't you talk? We know you're not a gorilla. And it's too early for trick or treat."

The man's eyes darted furtively between the four young girls.

"Maybe he can't talk," Dina said.

Gwen took a step closer to the man and he cowered as if he were scared of her. "Don't be afraid. Can you talk, mister?"

There was something sad about the man, Gwen thought. Maybe he was handicapped. Maybe he needed help. She should go get her mother.

"I think I'm going to get sick," Mary said before she ran. She always had a weak stomach. Gwen sat next to her in Ms. Janice's class in first grade and watched her throw up at least three times a week when she was at her desk. It was enough to make Gwen hurl.

Turning to Haley and Dina, Gwen said, "I think something's wrong with him. Maybe he's lost and needs help."

Dina had cupped her hands over her face in a vain attempt to keep the stink at bay. "My Uncle Benny does all kinds of weird things because he doesn't know any better. Sometimes, he goes for walks and people have to find him and bring him home."

"Are you lost?" Gwen asked him. The man stayed perfectly still, only his eyes moving. Something was definitely wrong. Her mother could help him. "You want to come with me?" She reached her hand out. The man stared at her open palm but didn't move.

"I'm telling my mother," Haley said and turned around and shouted, "Mom!"

Oh no. Haley's mom was mean. She was going to yell at Haley for talking to the man and get Gwen's mother all crazy so she would be mad, too, even though he obviously wasn't exactly right.

The man flinched when Haley cried out.

"Come on," Gwen said. She laid her hand on his arm. The fur on his suit wasn't soft. It felt more like a Brillo pad. "You'll be okay. Trust me."

She had to tug a little to get the man to stand. When he rose to his full height, which was really tall, Haley's mother, who had been waddling over, shrieked. "Kids! Get away from him!"

Just great. Now all of the other mothers and the one father who came to the park with his son all the time were looking at them. Most of the moms started to get up from their seats.

The man in the gorilla suit stiffened.

"Just ignore her," Gwen said. "She's always loud."

Some of the kids who had been running around playing saw the huge costume and started screaming.

"He's just dressed up for Halloween," Gwen cried. She saw her mother from the corner of her eye start walking her way. "I think he's lost."

Haley's mom grabbed Haley by the wrist and pulled her hard. "What did I tell you about talking to strangers, young lady?" She cast a glaring eye at the man.

"I didn't talk to him. Gwen did." Haley loved to blame other people so she got in less trouble. Gwen hated it, but she understood. Haley's mom was like a charging bull when she got angry.

"Gwen?"

Her mother looked worried. Why was everyone acting so crazy? Gwen held onto the man. She could feel him trying to pull away.

"Mommy. Can you help him? I think he's scared now."

Not as scared as the other people in the park who were picking up their kids and streaming out of the front gate. She heard someone yell, "Call nine-one-one!"

Haley's mother hauled Haley and Dina away. Haley shouted, "But I didn't do anything!"

Gwen looked up at the man and saw the fear in his eyes.

"Gwen, honey, I need you to come to me," her mother said.

"That's what I was going to do," she said, trying to tug the man with her. He wouldn't budge. She couldn't blame him. Everyone was acting crazy.

Her mother got to within a few feet and stopped. She held her arms out. "Just you."

"But we have to help him."

Her mother swallowed loudly. "Ah…we will, baby. But first, I need you to come over here."

Gwen turned up to the man's costumed face and said, "I'm sorry. You stay right here."

She reluctantly let go and slowly walked toward her mother. As soon as she was within reach, her mother snatched her off her feet, pulling her to her chest.

"Ow, you're hurting me."

"I'm sorry. I'm sorry." She started backing away.

"Where are we going? We can't leave him here."

"Shh, shhh." Her mother stroked her hair. "He's…he's going to be just fine."

Gwen struggled to be free. "I don't want to be carried like a baby. Why is everybody being mean to him?"

"We're not mean," her mother replied, her voice all shaky and scared sounding. "We just…we just…"

The man looked at Gwen as she was being taken away and she would swear his mask changed, the lips and brow curling down. He almost looked sad.

"Jimmy, no!" a woman screeched.

Little Jimmy Dolan, a four-year old terror who was always getting into trouble and running from his mother so much that he was usually on a leash, was hustling back into the park, his feet keeping a soccer ball in front of him while he giggled.

Gwen's mother saw him and said, "Jimmy, go back outside and listen to your mother."

Jimmy didn't even pause. He just gave her that mischievous smile of his and kept on going.

The little boy had the big man's attention. Gwen was mad at Jimmy for distracting him. She was mad at everybody at the moment. This was not the way to start Halloween.

His mother came racing into the park, at least as much as she could race with that limp that she had.

"Don't do that, Jimmy," Gwen's mom warned him.

He pulled his right leg back and kicked the ball as hard as he could, which was remarkably forceful for the miniscule maniac. The ball lifted off the ground, taking to the air like a hawk and headed straight for the man.

Gwen's mother quickened her pace, heading for the exit.

The ball made a beeline right for the man's crotch. It thumped him pretty hard.

When he screamed, Gwen realized that was no man in a suit.

She shrieked in unison.

The creature lashed out and shattered the thick wooden planks of the back of the bench. Splinters filled the air. One of them stabbed Jimmy's arm. He recoiled and instantly started to cry, just in time for his mother to arrive.

The monster roared at Jimmy. His mother passed out, landing on her back. Gwen's mother plucked him from the ground and ran. Gwen watched in horror as the monster, howling in pain and rage, grabbed the link fence to the basketball court and pulled it from the bar with the ease of yanking a tablecloth off a table.

Gwen's vision of the angry creature bounced wildly as her mother sprinted out of the park. Jimmy's mother was flat out on the ground. She was lucky she hadn't been stepped on. The chorus of screaming rose from those who had stayed outside the gates to watch.

When the monster ripped the teeter-totter from its base and broke it over its knee, Gwen started to cry. That was her favorite part of the park.

Vito heard the screaming and stopped Shay by grabbing his shoulder. It didn't take a rocket scientist to know where it was coming from. He was sick to his stomach.

"Goddamn!"

Visions of innocent children being stomped by the bigfoot made him dizzy. Their blood was on his and Shay's hands. He was pretty sure he wouldn't be able to live with such a thing weighing on him every second of the day.

"They might have just spotted it and are scared," Shay said, as if he could read Vito's mind and assure them both that they weren't child murderers.

Then came the inhuman roar.

Then even more screeching, a choir of young and old losing their shit.

And worse yet, the distinctive sounds of wood and metal being destroyed.

They ran as fast as they could, clipping their arms into trees and nearly getting their feet tangled up in roots.

The bigfoot was in the playground, and from the sound of things, it was laying waste to everyone and everything in it. At that moment, Vito loathed himself. He despised Shay for getting him into this madness. Dreading what he was going to see once they cleared the trees, he thought, *if it wasn't for Meredith, I'd turn this rifle on myself after shooting that fucking thing.*

Not far to go, he braced himself for what was sure to be a horrendous, life altering sight.

Vito and Shay popped out of the woods and onto the worn path around the park's perimeter. The first thing Vito spotted was the crowd of people running across the street, fleeing the madness in the park. It reminded him of the scene in Jaws when everyone was desperately trying to get out of the water.

Vito raised his rifle, walking cautiously, steadily now, spying the interior of the park through the fence.

There it was, just past the basketball courts. The bigfoot was systematically ripping the swings off the bar, tossing the seats and chains high over its head and into the trees. It was huffing and baring its teeth, in an obvious rage.

"Oh, thank God," Shay said.

Vito took his eyes off the bigfoot and saw there were no bodies of children strewn about. However, there was an unconscious woman on the ground. When the bigfoot backhanded a bench, the two-by-four sailed up and dropped almost directly onto the woman's head.

"We have to get it before she gets squashed by shrapnel," Vito said.

"I think she's already dead," Shay said. They crept toward the front gate.

A woman's voice shouted, "They have guns!"

Vito couldn't tell from her tone if that was a good or a bad thing. Too bad this hadn't happened later in the day when the informal men's basketball leagues would fill the basketball courts. He was sure there'd be quite a few more guns on hand.

Eyeing the prone woman, Vito said, "We don't know for sure. We can't take a chance."

So far, the bigfoot was too wrapped up in its annihilation of the park to notice them. They had a pretty clear shot already. The only problem was, the woods directly behind the bigfoot were thin and there was a wide path that led to a field just ten yards back. Sure, most people had already headed for the hills, but there was still a chance someone was there within the trees, hiding, or maybe even filming the spectacle on their phone. If he or Shay missed, that bullet was going into those trees and possibly somebody. They had to get closer.

The bigfoot completed its mass destruction of the swings and now was caving in the jungle gym with its massive kicks and footfalls.

Vito tasted blood and realized he'd bitten the inside of his cheek hard enough to shred the pulpy flesh.

"Look," Shay whispered, pointing with the barrel of his gun. The woman had started to move, rocking from side to side and rubbing her forehead.

"Get her out of here," Vito said. "I'll distract it."

If he only felt as confident as he sounded.

The creature had its back to them. Shay ran over to the woman in a crouch and grabbed her arm. She looked at him woozily. He motioned for her to follow him out of the park. He had to help her up. When she focused on the bigfoot, she swooned and nearly took another dive. Shay held onto her tight around her waist and made an almost three-legged walk out of the park.

Vito's knees knocked. Everything in his body was screaming at him to run like hell.

The bigfoot was massive and obviously furious beyond measure.

I suppose I would be too if I had been drugged, taken from my home and left in a smelly old shed. Not that the musty odor of the shed could compete with the musk of the sasquatch.

The sound of an approaching siren flooded him with relief.

The cops! Let them take care of this. Clean up his and Shay's mess. At least no one had been hurt. They wouldn't get their fifteen minutes of fame, but at least they wouldn't have to live with crushing guilt. A park could be rebuilt.

The bigfoot must have heard the siren too, because it whirled around and came eye-to-eye with Vito.

"Fuck me sideways."

What Vito saw in those eyes was something not animal, not human. This creature was somewhere in between, or better yet, something beyond the two. He was overcome with a desperate need to take a shit. His rifle trembled in his hands.

For a brief moment, he felt as if the bigfoot were deciding whether to tear his arms off or run. The air was redolent with menace and indecision.

The sirens were getting closer. Shay yelled something to Vito, but he couldn't make out the words through the thrumming in his ears.

Just shoot it!

Even Vito could miss a center mass shot from this distance.

The bigfoot wouldn't take its eyes off of Vito. It lived in the woods and it must have known the damage a gun could do. Vito would swear it was both daring him to shoot and not to pull the trigger. His finger feathered along the trigger, but he couldn't bring himself to apply the needed pressure.

He heard he *whoop-whoop* of an approaching cop car.

The second Vito lowered his rifle, the bigfoot took off at a sprint back into the woods. It barreled through the back opening in the fence and plunged into the trees. It should have made a ton of noise in its retreat, but in seconds it was swallowed by silence.

"Why didn't you shoot it?"

Vito didn't realize he'd been staring open mouthed at the woods. Shay shook him hard. "You had him dead to rights."

"I…I…"

Tugging on his sleeve, Shay said, "Never mind. We have to get out of here before the cops swarm this place. Let's go."

He practically dragged Vito back into the woods. Vito took a quick glance behind him and saw a police car come to a skidding stop outside the playground. Two uniforms jumped out, reaching for their guns when they saw the level of destruction.

Vito and Shay crashed through the woods like a pair of bulldozers. Shay kept cursing about how they had missed what might have been their best shot to get the bigfoot.

Vito had been struck temporarily mute, but his brain was on fire.

He wasn't sure they should shoot the bigfoot anymore. There was an emotional intelligence behind the creature's dark eyes. That almost telepathic exchange between them had indelibly changed Vito's course of action. It could have easily harmed or killed a good number of children and parents as it tore the playground apart. But, it hadn't. Something had set it off, yet it had enough restraint to focus its anger on the inanimate.

They were not going to shoot the bigfoot at all.

What they needed to do now was save it from those who would.

CHAPTER TWELVE

The sasquatch zipped through the trees with amazing speed and agility. For a creature so large, it was as light on its feet as a ghost when it needed to be.

It stopped at the edge of a clearing where there was a large path with so many of the shiny things that moved faster than it ever could. It pulled back into the trees and kept running. Its hands and feet hurt from smashing and punching and kicking the playground to smithereens.

For a moment back there, it had been at peace for the first time since waking up in the night. The small things made it happy, almost comforted. It liked the small things, especially the one that had touched its arm.

But then the big things started to make bad noises, and the little things got scared, their pheromones changing in an instant and giving the bigfoot cause for alarm.

And then there was the pain when the small thing hit it with the round thing.

The bigfoot did not like pain. Nothing set off its temper like pain.

As it ran, it recalled the image of the big thing that came, holding the stick that was very, very bad. The bigfoot knew the only way to stop if from using the stick was to intimidate it. And it had worked. Though there was something about the big thing that seemed different than the others it had seen in its home.

It was the closest the creature had ever gotten to one of the big things. It had watched many from afar before. Enough to know that when they came with those sticks, especially when the darkness came early and the temperature dropped, horrible things happened. The animals the bigfoot depended on to eat to prepare for the cold and white fell when the sticks made their noises at them. How often had the bigfoot watched groups of big things carry its food away, its stomach grumbling loud enough that it often had to disappear so the big things couldn't hear.

Some cold and white times, the bigfoot grew very weak and barely made it to the warm and bright times. On those days, when it was hidden in a safe place, it would think of all the big things and their loud sticks and the food that was taken from the bigfoot's home. It did not hate the big things because hate was something it knew nothing of, but it did wish they would go away with their sticks.

It stopped at another clearing that was again filled with the fast shiny things. There were very little trees here and too many places where the shiny things ran.

The sasquatch heard the big things in the trees. They weren't close now, but they would be.

Across one path was the place that was almost like home but had the many rocks sticking up from the ground. It did not want to go back there, especially if there was a chance that ear-splitting sound was still in there.

But just beyond that was another place like home, only without the rocks. There were trees, so many trees. It called to the bigfoot.

The only problem was the fast, shiny things. How could it get past them?

Brush crunched in the lessening distance.

The big things were coming with their sticks.

Hunkering low, the bigfoot waited, wondering what to do.

At first, Shay had been mad at Vito for freezing up back there. He wished Vito were the one who had to practically carry the woman out of the park.

The more he thought about it as they followed the pungent scent of the bigfoot through the woods, the less angry he became. The creature wasn't far. It could be just up ahead, waiting, watching, ready to pounce. If Shay was honest with himself, he wasn't sure what he would do if it plopped down from the trees like a damn Predator.

"Unless our noses fall off, there's no way we can lose it now," Shay said.

"You also said it was dead, so I'm not putting my money on you," Vito replied.

"I never was good at the track."

"Tell me about it. Whatever happened to the luck of the Irish?"

Shay thought he heard something, stopped and pressed his back against a tree. His mouth was so dry, he thought he might choke if he tried to swallow. When thirty seconds passed without a sound, he exhaled and got back to tracking the sasquatch. "My grandfather lost most of his paychecks on the ponies. We have luck in the family. It's just the bad kind."

"We should probably stop and call the authorities," Vito said breathlessly. "This is crazy being out here. You saw what it did to the playground. What are we possibly going to do if we corner it again?"

"Take it down."

Vito shook his head. "No, we're not, bro. You know it, and I know it. And at this point, I'm not sure if shooting it isn't the same as killing a person, if not legally, at least morally."

"It's an animal. Just because it walks upright doesn't make it the same as you and me."

"I'm not saying it is. But you didn't look right into its eyes like I did. It's not an animal. And it's not like us at all. No matter what, it doesn't deserve to die. It's our fault it's out here."

The sounds of traffic crept into the woods. They were close to the end of the park.

"If we call the cops now," Shay said, "they'll first think we're crackpots and hang up. When more people see this thing and send proof to the police, they'll probably arrest us for endangering the public."

"I hate to say it, but you're right."

"I'm still waiting for Katie to utter those same words," Shay said, smiling for the first time that morning.

"You know what we have to do then, right?"

"Honestly, I'm not sure anymore."

Vito said, "This thing is too big and wild to not be found. When it is, we have to be there to stop it from being slaughtered. Because that's what's going to happen. It's a powerful, confused, maybe angry creature, for lack of a better word, surrounded by, like, a million people. The first priority for the police is to protect the people."

Shay stopped and turned to Vito. "So what, you want us to play human shield for this thing?"

Vito stood his ground. "If it comes to it, something like that, yeah."

What Shay wanted to do was tell Vito he'd lost his mind. The incident in the playground had shaken him up. He just needed a moment to regain his senses.

But he'd known Vito all his life, and that look on his friend's face said this was the hill he was willing to die on.

Literally.

"So, we're going to try to play heroes for a cryptid that probably wants to eat our faces off?"

"We are. And it doesn't. And before you open your big mouth, just trust me."

Shay resumed walking. "Right. Well, this just made today even more interesting."

"Think of it as good karma."

They went the rest of the way in silence. The now familiar bigfoot musk got strong enough to make them pull the collars of their shirts over their noses. It could be anywhere. Shay's neck hurt from swiveling his head from side to side, up and down, anticipating a bigfoot strike at any moment.

You didn't corner a wild animal and not expect consequences.

Vito says it's not an animal. Boy, do I hope he's right.

He could see the Major Deegan through the trees. Traffic was starting to slow down on the south side, which eventually took riders to places like the George Washington Bridge, Yankee Stadium and Hunts Point Market. There must have been an accident down the line. Jerome Avenue ran parallel to the parkway. A minivan sped past that was decorated with eyelashes on the headlights and a big pair of red lips on the front grill. An upright skeleton had been strapped to the roof, its arm raised and right hand fluttering in the wind as if it were waving at everyone.

Shay kept forgetting it was Halloween. It was an easy thing to do when you were tracking a bigfoot in the last place in the world a bigfoot should be.

His attention captured by the minivan, he didn't see the flipping branch hurtling toward his head. Only when it smashed against a tree did he react, ducking and shouting something that may or may not have been English. Another tree branch came at them fast enough to whistle through the air.

"Jesus, Mary and Joseph!" Shay cried shielding his head with his arms. He dropped to the ground and rolled to his left. Vito did the same, rolling to his right. More and more branches whooshed overhead.

"Thing's got a cannon for an arm," Vito said.

"Get the Yankees to sign him up…after we get the hell out of here."

It must have run out of branches, because the rocks came next. One pinged off Shay's elbow, sending bright sparks of pain to his cerebrum. Quickly recovering, he found a stone of his own and chucked it in the general direction of the incoming rocks.

"What the hell are you doing?" Vito said.

Shay found another and let it fly just as a rock missed his left ear by centimeters. The close call sent him back to bellying up to the ground. "You throw shit at me, I'm going to throw stuff at you."

"I think it's just telling us not to come any closer."

"Message received. I hope it's getting mine." He blindly tossed a stone the size of his palm. He heard it knock into a tree.

"Maybe if we just…"

Vito was cut off by the screeching of tires and scent of burning rubber. A split-second later, the crashing started.

CHAPTER THIRTEEN

Vito was on his feet before Shay, running as fast as he could until he smacked into the fence. There were multiple car wrecks on Jerome Avenue in both directions. People were getting out of their cars not to argue with one another, but to turn and point at the blurry figure just before it dipped into the trees in the adjacent section of Van Cortlandt Park.

"Man, I hope no one is hurt," Vito said. He scanned the interiors of the cars, looking for anyone that looked like they needed immediate medical attention. He was Red Cross certified and ready to finally use those skills.

"I'll bet they're more freaked out than anything," Shay replied. "When's the last time you saw a pile up like that around here without people going at each other's throats?"

Vito stepped back, suddenly aware that he was holding a rifle and within the sightline of over a dozen confused people and growing. "It went into the park."

"Of course it did. A whole lot more ground to cover over there."

Police sirens sounded off close by. Vito would bet they were in the cemetery and heard the tremendous crunch of metal.

"Let's go back to my truck. We can't walk across the road like this."

Shay kicked the fence. "We also can't get from here to there with all those cars in the way. Unless we ditch the guns and go into the park unarmed."

As much as Vito was sure he didn't want to shoot the bigfoot, a part of him would feel a hell of a lot safer with a gun, especially seeing how the creature kicked the shit out of the playground. Going in defenseless was suicide and he had Meredith and Danielle to consider.

"We just have to wait it out, then," Vito said.

"It's going to take at least an hour to unsnarl that mess. We don't have that kind of time to waste."

Vito looked up at the clear blue sky, which was in stark contrast to the grayness they were wading through on terra firma. "I think I know how we can walk right past everyone without getting a second look."

They peeled away from the area by the gate when two cop cars arrived on the scene.

"Oh, and what would that be?" Shay asked as they walked quickly, heading for where Vito had parked his truck.

Vito grinned. "It's Halloween. We just need to dress the part so the guns look like part of the costume."

"I'm beginning to feel like we're not mentally fit to make logical decisions anymore."

"Hey, you bring a bigfoot to the Bronx, you have to expect shit to get weird."

When they emerged from the woods, the old man was no longer on the bench, though there was a prodigious amount of pigeon shit on the green painted wood. A typical thank you from the local rats with wings. They hopped in Vito's truck and were piling out in front of his house two minutes later.

"What have you guys been up to?" Danielle said. She sat on the couch reading a People magazine. She eyed them suspiciously when she noted the rifles in their hands.

"I was over at Shay's cleaning our guns," Vito said, hating to lie to his wife but knowing he didn't have time to explain the deep shit they'd gotten themselves into.

"You guys. Be careful with that. I can see you shooting each other by accident before a deer. I hate guns."

"Very funny."

Vito tried to leave the living room but Danielle said, "You hear all those sirens? I went outside but can't see what's going on. Sounded like a huge car wreck."

"I think it's on the Deegan," Shay said, "Sunday drivers is a real thing."

Danielle set the magazine on the couch cushion. "Yeah, but I heard sirens before that. It's like they moved mischief night to mischief day."

"Everyone's nuts on Halloween," Vito said, hurrying up the stairs. In the second floor hallway, he pulled the cord that opened the hatch and collapsible steps to the attic.

The unfinished attic was stacked with boxes, most of them marked with tags like Christmas Lights, Meredith's Baby Clothes, Grandma E's Stuff, Books. Vito went to the back corner, stooping to avoid cracking his skull on the low, pitched ceiling. He found three plastic bins filled with Halloween costumes and ripped the lids open.

Shay sat on Meredith's old bicycle and watched him tear through the boxes, tossing Disney Princess pastel costumes aside. "What's Danielle going to say when we walk past her all dressed up like we're going trick or treating?"

Vito stopped for a moment and looked at Shay as if he had an IQ hovering somewhere near a housefly's. "We're not getting changed up here. We'll wait until we're in the car."

"Okay. What if she asks why we're going out with the costumes?"

Vito opened his mouth, and then closed it. Shay had a point. "We could tell her we're donating them to the White Owl. The bar is always taking up a collection for the Irish."

"That's because we take care of our own," Shay said. "Unlike you Italians, who when they say they're going to take care of their own, it means someone is about to disappear."

Digging through another box, Vito said, "You're a freaking comedian, you know that? Well, wait until you see what I have for you."

"I'm actually kinda worried."

Vito removed a packaged witch costume – Danielle had worn it to a party before they'd had Meredith – and found what he was looking for. "Aha!"

He took out the brown jacket and pants with the big brown and maroon hat pinned to the jacket.

"What the hell is that?" Shay asked.

"I was Elmer Fudd for an office party about fifteen years ago. I wear this, my rifle is a prop so I can hunt some wabbits."

Shay ran his hand over his face. "Sweet Jesus. And what am I supposed to be?"

Vito took great delight in showing his friend. The gray and white full body costume came with an oversized, plastic carrot.

Shay got off the bike. "Oh no. I am not dressing up like Bugs Bunny to track a bigfoot. What if it kills me? You think I want to go out looking like that?"

Vito tossed the knock-off Bugs Bunny costume at Shay. "If you die, I don't think you'll really care if you're dressed like Nicki Minaj."

Shay let the rabbit costume fall to the floor. "Not a chance. You have to have something else in there."

"Sure. You want to be a slutty biker or the Little Mermaid? Take your pick."

Vito could feel precious time slipping away. There was no time to dicker over this. "We have to get hopping if we expect to find your bigfoot."

Shay followed him down the rickety steps. "Get to hopping. Very funny."

"I have to find something to laugh at."

They lucked out for once that morning. Danielle was not in the living room when they left. Vito heard her downstairs doing the laundry. They got in the truck, drove around the block and changed while parked on East 233rd Street.

"I hate you, you know that, right?" Shay said, his face sticking out of the furry rabbit head.

"Hate is just love on bad day, bro," Vito said. He drove over to Indian Field and they got out to inspect the traffic situation. There were multiple cop cars now and three ambulances. They'd definitely have to walk through it all to get to the park.

Jerome Avenue was utter chaos. Now people were upset about the accident, but there was also a bit of hysteria over what had caused the accident.

"I'm telling you, it was a gorilla," a man said to one of the officers. "You should check with the Bronx Zoo. I'll bet one of them got out."

"I think it was a bear," a woman interjected. "Walking on its hind legs."

"That thing was too fast to be a bear," another man said. "I don't know what that was."

"Great," a middle-aged woman wearing a pant suit practically screamed. "You wrecked my new BMW over a bear or a gorilla. My lawyer is gonna have a field day with you assholes."

"I need you to calm down, miss," a young cop said.

"And I need you to arrest these clowns for causing all of…all of this!"

Vito cringed as he listened in on their conversations and saw the shape the cars were in. If he and Shay were forced to pay for the repairs of the cars and playground, they'd been in debt until they were five-hundred years old.

The anger and confusion worked in their favor. No one even batted an eye in their direction. They quickly hustled past the melee and weaved around the cars log-jammed on Jerome Avenue. The people in the parked cars gave them plenty of looks, but it was mostly the *look at those idiots* variety. Vito could live with that.

Someone leaned out of their open window and called out to Shay, "What's up, doc?"

"Your mother's sister," Shay curtly replied.

The man called Shay something awful as they walked away, getting to the other side of the road and headed for the entrance to the park. Vito, who had been carrying both rifles, handed one to the bunny-clad Shay as they hopped the metal bar that prevented cars from entering. This time of year, the park should be empty.

Save for a very perturbed bigfoot.

Shay pulled the top part of the costume back with a quick yank on the ears. "You're enjoying this. I can tell."

Vito pursed his lips to keep from laughing and shook his head. "I have no idea what you're talking about."

"Whatever. Remember, if we find it, call Animal Control and just wait. I'm sure they've heard there's some kind of animal in the area. At least they shouldn't dismiss us as kooks. That is, until they get a look at us." Shay took the lead, going off the trail and into the brush.

Vito tapped Shay on the shoulder.

"What?"

"Remember," Vito said. "Be vewy, vewy quiet."

"Fuck off."

CHAPTER FOURTEEN

Exhaustion finally took over.

The bigfoot crawled into a cluster of brambles, making sure it could not be seen. The fast moving things on the path had frightened it terribly. What was worse was the sounds they made as the bigfoot ran through them. Its heart was still beating mightily against its chest.

It chewed on leaves as it lay in a ball, trying to settle down. It was so hungry, but there didn't seem to be much here to eat. At least not enough to satisfy its caloric needs. Add to that the increasing stress and it was nearing a breaking point.

Normally a creature of the dusk and night, it was not accustomed to moving about so freely in the day. Everything was off. It couldn't trust its own instincts.

What it couldn't resist was the hard pull of sleep.

It felt safe, at least for the moment. There were no scents of the large things on the wind. If they did come, the bigfoot would sense them immediately and awaken. It was an incredibly fine tuned defense system that had kept it safe all its life.

It wouldn't get to rest for very long.

Joey knew that the promise of a little weed would get Ellie out of her house. The girl loved to smoke. He heard there were other things she loved to do, too. He hoped to have confirmation very soon.

"I'm cold," Ellie said, stepping cautiously over a gnarled tree limb. It was obvious by her face that she did not like being in the woods. She was kind of a priss and very self aware of her hotness. Joey figured she was worried she might mess her hair up or dirty her expensive sneakers out here.

But he had a couple of joints in his pocket and had overheard her tell Stacy Rafferty outside Frank's Pizza parlor yesterday that she was broke and dying to get high.

Opportunity knocked Joey over the head and he was answering it as quickly as he could. In fact, he'd been so excited about today's prospects that he'd taken several zans to settle his nerves. That and the two Percocets he'd popped on the way to her house would have had a normal person drooling in their soup, but Joey was no rank amateur.

"It's not that bad out," Joey said, never thinking of offering her his oversized Dallas Cowboys jacket.

She stopped and twirled around to face him with the same grace she had on the football field in her cheerleader uniform. "Look, this is as far as I'm going, J. Let's just smoke and go home." She wrapped her arms around her chest. Joey would bet anything her nipples were hard as rocks under those arms.

He kept walking. "You saw all those cops out there. I don't wanna take a chance."

"I really don't think they're going to smell your skunk weed from all the way over there."

She was right. They could smoke a blunt as fat as his thigh and the five-oh would never know.

He was trekking a little deeper into the woods because he was looking for a small clearing that also gave them cover. Not for the smoking. But for the other thing.

Ellie griped with each step, but she wasn't leaving, either. They had a huge science test this coming week and he knew she was anal about her grades. Like she couldn't get into a good college if she didn't get an A on one stupid test. She needed to chill out and knew it. And he knew it.

He spied a perfect spot just ahead. There was just enough room for the two of them to get comfortable and plenty of foliage and shit to keep them from prying eyes. "How about there?" he asked, pointing.

"Fine. As long as we can stop walking."

He took one of the joints out of his pocket and waved it in front of her.

"This better not be a bunch of nasty seeds and oregano," Ellie said.

"No way. This shit is dope. You're gonna get high AF."

Ellie sneered at him. "Would you please stop talking like that? You're not some bad ass street thug."

"Whatever."

She held her hand out and he gave her the joint.

"Please tell me you have a lighter," she said.

"I'm not an idiot."

Her eyes told him she seriously doubted that. No matter. After today, he was the one who would have one up on her.

"Here." He gave her his lighter, a cheap Bic that he'd swiped from his mother's dresser.

Ellie wasted no time firing it up and inhaling deeply. She started coughing and her eyes watered. "Whoa, that's strong."

Joey smiled. "I told you. Hang with me more often, you'll get used to the best."

She took another toke and handed it over to him. He kept it pinched between his thumb and index finger.

"You're not gonna smoke?" Ellie asked. Her eyes had gone as glassy as a still pond.

"I will," he said. "Ladies first, you know."

He offered her the joint and she took it, but not without a little side-eye. "Yeah, sure."

After the third toke, she started to weave a bit. Her eyes rolled up and she coughed hard into her hand. "Wow. What's the name of this stuff? It tastes different."

Now, Joey wasn't going to tell her he'd laced the joint. There was a chance she'd remember this moment and he couldn't risk it.

When it looked like she was about to fall, he swooped in like a vulture, wrapped his arm around her and pulled her close. Her breasts mashed against his chest. He let his hand 'accidentally' slip until it rested on one of her ass cheeks.

"You okay?" he asked.

Her head rolled on her neck as if it were broken. What she replied to him was indecipherable gibberish.

Joey eased them both to the ground, his other hand roving up to her neck and back down until he cupped her breast. "You feeling better now?"

"Gnnn…offa me…"

Joey leaned in and kissed her neck, tasting the fruity soap she'd showered with.

"You're gonna be just fine. Just sit back and take a little nap."

When he tried to put his hand up her shirt, she pulled herself together somewhat and grabbed his wrist. "Wha da fuck are you doin?"

"Nothing. Shhh. Shhh. You're dreaming."

He went for her breasts again and she blurted, "No" before her eyelids fluttered.

Settling her onto her back, he tamped out the spiked joint and lit the other one for himself. He fumbled with his belt, the joint clamped between his teeth. He hadn't counted for the drug to hit her this hard. No matter. He was still going to get what he came for. It didn't matter if she was passed out. In fact, it was probably better. Ellie treated him like he didn't exist at school. Joey hated to be ignored, dismissed, stepped around like he was road kill. Stuck up bitch had this coming for years.

The struggle to get her jeans off woke her up again. This time, she managed to let out one hell of a shriek. It was strong enough to kill his boner.

"Shut up," he hissed.

She screamed again, though he could tell that she was having a hard time focusing.

Joey slapped a hand over her mouth. She tried to bite him, but it was so weak, it was almost cute.

Ellie feebly slapped him away, but he pressed on. He removed his shirt. She swiped at him, her fake nails raking down his chest, opening up a trio of deep scratches.

"You bitch!"

Tiny droplets of blood trickled down his chest.

He punched her in the stomach, knocking the wind and most of the fight from her.

Time to seal the deal.

The high wail catapulted the bigfoot from its brief slumber. There was a curious smell in the air. It heard more wails, but the others were softer. To the creature, it sounded very close to the small things back at the other place.

It rose silently from its hiding place, following the sound and smell.

With preternatural insight, it managed to avoid any crunching leaves as it stalked the woods without even looking down. A flock of birds resting atop a denuded tree exploded into the air as it passed by.

It didn't take long to find the pair on the ground.

One of the big things was on top of another. It couldn't tell what they were doing. The one that sounded like one of the little things flopped like a fish that had been pulled out of the water.

Sniffing the air, the bigfoot's mouth instantly watered.

The electric smell of copper was coming from the one on top. The sasquatch needed meat. Where there was that copper smell, there was meat, and strength.

Normally, the bigfoot would do everything in its power to avoid the big things, even if they radiated the scent that it craved. But in this place, it seemed as if there were big things everywhere. It survived not by routine and complacency, but through adaptation.

Its stomach was commanding it to adapt to this new situation immediately.

Joey tugged on his cock but nothing was happening. If Ellie would just shut the fuck up and go to sleep, he could get to where he needed to be. He hoped he hadn't taken too many pills. That would truly suck.

"What the fuck's that smell?"

He cringed at the pungent odor that came from nowhere.

He heard rustling behind some bushes and turned around. An enormous, hairy monster launched itself straight for him. Joey tried to scream but nothing came out.

With his hand still gripping his limp noodle, the creature grabbed him by the back of his neck and lifted him off the ground. His feet pedaled in the air. The pressure on his neck was the most intense pain he'd ever felt.

The creature turned him around until they were practically eye to eye. Its face was like tanned leather, its nose wide and nearly flat, lips and gums like black licorice. But the teeth, good God, they were sharp and yellow with jagged edges, perfectly made for ripping through flesh.

Ellie shouted something, but Joey no longer cared about her.

Holy shit, he thought, *it's a fucking bigfoot*!

He could be totally tripping, but that increasing pain would have brought him right out of any high. Joey loved monster movies and documentaries on strange creatures and knew a bigfoot when he saw one. Despite the exceeding terror of the situation he found himself in, his mind raced, wondering if he'd ever heard of a sasquatch sighting in the Bronx. Maybe when the land was populated by Indians, well before Columbus stumbled upon America. No way could one be living all this time in Van Cortlandt Park. So, where the fuck did this thing come from?

It sounded as if the bigfoot was chewing on rocks. Joey quickly came to realize that was the popping of the bones in his neck. He fought to drag in a breath, to get the creature to let him go. His fists glanced off skin and bone that may as well have been iron.

Snarling, the bigfoot lifted him even higher. When Joey's chest was level with its face, it snapped forward and sunk its teeth so deep into his flesh, his ribs turned to dust.

The explosion of pain severed Joey's ability to fight back. His arms and legs went limp, jittering when the bigfoot slurped deeply, sucking Joey's blood and mashed muscle into its grisly maw.

I'm being eaten by a bigfoot. How is this even possible?

Joey let out a strangled chuckle a second before his neck and throat collapsed from the bigfoot's grip.

Lying on the cold ground, dumbstruck with terror, Ellie gave up screaming and passed out.

The bigfoot drank and ate until blood bubbled up its esophagus and splattered on the leaves by its feet.

No longer needing the big thing, it tossed the husk of its body aside.

The other one hadn't moved.

It would bury them both so it could come back for them later when its hunger returned.

Dragging the dead one deeper into the cover of the trees, the bigfoot saw the sky tilt and had to stop and take a knee. Something was wrong. Things looked...strange. Even the sound of a crying bird overhead sounded off.

The bigfoot fought to regain some semblance of equilibrium, but it was a losing battle. With a system flooded by Joey's pharmacologically poisoned blood and viscera, the bigfoot, unaccustomed to anything but the purest meat, let the body slip from its fingers and forced itself to walk, wrapped in a dull fog.

CHAPTER FIFTEEN

Shay felt like a horse's ass traipsing through the woods dressed like Bugs Bunny. The headpiece bounced off his back as he walked. The only saving grace was that no one was out and about to see him. It was amazing how fear of humiliation was able to throw his worries about being killed by a bigfoot to the back seat. He wasn't sure what that said about him and frankly didn't care.

The woods were a little deeper in this section of the park, but he could still hear the traffic on the Deegan. Not too far from the highway was the Mosholu Parkway, which cut through the heart of the Bronx.

At one point, he thought he heard a girl scream. He and Vito stopped in mid-stride, fingers gliding onto their triggers. The unmistakable grumbling of a car passing by on Jerome Avenue with what sounded like a gaggle of giddy teens howling at the Halloween wind set them at ease, at least for the moment.

It had been an abnormally warm fall, so there were more leaves on the trees and bushes than usual, giving the bigfoot plenty of places to hide. If they'd had just a handful of colder nights, the search would have been so much easier.

It felt as if they'd been walking for hours and Shay was pretty sure he'd seen that mossy log before, which meant they were going in circles. He took out his phone and went to check the news feed. But first, it was impossible not to see the missed calls from his wife and a last text that said – Where r u?

He'd kept his phone on silent while they searched for the squatch. If he didn't answer her soon, the texts would take on a decidedly angry tone and truth be told, Shay was more frightened of a pissed off Katie than any bigfoot. He jumped to his browser and searched for any strange stories.

"Somebody murdered bagpipers in Woodlawn Cemetery," he said, his thumb scrolling the screen as he speed-read the breaking report.

"What?" Vito sidled up to him and read over his shoulder. "'Police are still investigating'. Doesn't look like they have a suspect."

"You know what that means."

Vito removed the Elmer Fudd hat and wiped his sweaty head down with the sleeve of his jacket. "Anything about the park?"

Shay leaned against a tree and typed in a few searches. There was nothing hitting the news yet, but on social media he found a couple of posts about vandals wrecking Woodlawn Park. His heart skipped a beat when he spotted a tweet that said –

Some kind of monster is in the park and this isn't a Halloween prank. Tell me what you see! #WTFisthat?

Attached to the tweet was a hazy photo of the creature. It had its back to the person who took the picture through the rails of the front fence. The bigfoot was tearing the fence pole by the swings up from the ground. Because it was in motion, the camera didn't get a clear shot of it. Only a couple of fools who had carried the damn thing all the way from Minnewaska State Park would know exactly what had been captured in the photo.

"That can't be the only picture that was taken," Vito said.

"Not with the way these mothers snap away with their phones on a boring day, no." Shay tapped in a few more searches, looking for any other reports of strange goings on in their area. "It's only a matter of time before big and hairy is all over the news with photos and police sketches."

They resumed walking and came to the blacktop of a parking lot. A baseball field was on the other side of the lot. It was a big, open space. Definitely not a prime bigfoot hideout. They turned around and trudged on, crossing the road that led to the lot a couple of minutes later.

"Jesus, I need a drink," Shay said.

"After last night, I thought I'd be good for a week break, but I'm with you."

"Hold this." Shay handed his rifle over to Vito and unzipped his rabbit costume. He stepped out of it and tossed it over a branch. "I'm not wearing that thing anymore. Besides, I have to shed a tear for the old country. No peeking."

Shay urinated on the base of a tree.

"You could have at least tried to be a little modest," Vito said.

"Screw modesty when you're always a second away from getting your head lopped off by a sasquatch." He finished and zipped up. "I say we pack it in."

Last night, all he could think of was the money they would make by revealing their discovery to the world. Today, what he wanted most was to be with his wife and daughter and forget that they had ever found the creature. Vito was right that they had a level of responsibility for the beast. But it was obviously very good at hiding. And if it wanted to hide and not slaughter bagpipers or demolish things for a while, Shay was perfectly okay with letting it do so, at least for a few hours. It would be getting dark soon and trick or treating would begin. If he didn't take Caitlin out for candy, he would be in deeper dog doo than a may fly at a shit picnic.

"I think we should keep looking," Vito said.

"It might not even be here."

"There's no way it crossed the Deegan. And I'm pretty sure it wouldn't go back into the cemetery with all the activity going on in there."

Shay held up a finger. "That cemetery is like fifty times bigger than this section of the park. If I was a bigfoot, I might go there. The cops are gone by now."

Vito shook his head. "I think it's too smart for that. It knows when to move on."

"And you get this from that one look you shared back at the park?"

"Yeah, I do," Vito replied with no uncertainty. "At the other end of this, you have the Mosholu Golf Course and the filtration plant. I think it'll avoid those areas. I'm telling you, it's trapped here."

"And you and I will be trapped in divorce court if we stay here much longer."

"But this is our freaking mess."

"A mess that is way too big for us to clean up. We're like Mrs. O'Leary's cow in the great Chicago Fire. You can't really blame the cow for being a stupid animal, now can you?"

Vito looked at him with utter exasperation. "I'll enjoy seeing that as your defense at our trial. Cow man too dumb for prison."

With a roll of his eyes, Shay grabbed the bunny costume and headed back the way they'd come. "We're not heroes, Vito. We're the dumbasses in the red shirts on Star Trek. I'm surprised we've even made it this far without getting eighty-sixed. We'll come back for it. The experts believe bigfoots are nocturnal anyway."

"Is there such a thing as a bigfoot expert?"

"There's science kinda guys on TV that say they are," Shay admitted rather sheepishly.

Vito kicked a rock and sent it flying. He was clearly exasperated, but Shay could see he was also coming around to his line of thinking. When Danielle was mad, the whole neighborhood knew it. "So, you're gonna come back out here when it's pitch black?"

Shay swallowed hard. "Or, we can wait until there's another sighting and haul ass. Look, when it comes to hide and seek, we're rank amateurs next to this thing. We can only hope the same dumb luck that dropped it in our laps will do it again. Come on. Trick or treating awaits."

Vito reluctantly agreed and they found the road that led out of the park.

At one point, Shay thought he heard footsteps off in the distance. He dismissed them because they were too loud and obvious to be the bigfoot. The thing may have weighed as much as a dead donkey, but it floated like a moth when it wanted to.

It would show up again. Of that he was sure.

The question was where, and when.

And would he and Vito be able to save it from a horrible end?

The more he thought about it, the less he believed that was at all possible.

The bigfoot had walked for a spell, bumping into tree trunks and tripping over deadfall. It had never felt this exhausted before. It managed to find a clump of greenery and dig a hiding hole where it fell into a disturbed sleep. Frightening images flashed through its slumbering brain. This was the furthest from a restful nap. It was more like a feverish semi-consciousness that did little to replenish the creature's strength.

When it awoke, the sun was sinking below the horizon. Cold beads of sweat speckled its face, soaked its flesh and fur.

It lay still for a long moment, feeling both sick and something else that was not within its experience. When it sat up, it was still hampered by vertigo and an uneasy interpretation of everything around it.

Move. It needed to move.

When it had eaten bad berries in the past, walking had always made it feel better. Walking meant surviving, whereas lying about in misery was akin to death. Not that the bigfoot fully understood the concept of misery or death.

So, it walked, unsteadily at first, still weaving, but also stopping to stare at leaves or the sky or the ground, seeing everything shifting and swirling, colors bleeding into one another. Even when the night took hold, the sasquatch could still detect colors all around it, a kaleidoscope of unnerving intensity.

It didn't even notice when it left the woods and stepped barefoot onto the paved parking lot. When it did pause to see what it was walking on, it saw a roiling sea of blackness. This terrified the bigfoot. It ran recklessly, bullying through a wire fence and onto the baseball field. Dust kicked up as it fled the angry dark waters until it was back within the trees, but not for long.

Suddenly, there were no more trees and the ground undulated, which only increased the bigfoot's loss of equilibrium. It fell into a sand trap, winding itself. The bigfoot lay on its back and looked up into the stars, seeing them more as melting icicles, heading for the ground.

The Mosholu Golf Course was closed for golfers, which meant Jefferson Banks could get started. He settled into the worn leather seat of the riding mower and started the engine. Slapping on noise canceling headphones, he pulled out of the shed and onto the course, the bright light he'd installed himself on the mower bouncing crazily.

Groundskeeping was done at night so the crew didn't interfere with the golfers during the day. Jefferson had always been a night owl, so this was a sort of dream job. He'd work until one in the morning, then stop at Henry's Bar for a quick pint on the way home to his apartment on Bainbridge Avenue. He had a crew of three, though they were down to two tonight because Whitey had called in sick with a stomach flu. No matter. Driving and mowing under the moon, with the sweet smell of freshly cut grass, was an absolute oasis considering they were surrounded by a bustling city that was pretty nasty in parts. Why, just outside the entrance to the golf course was the subway and a miles long strip of stores and loud cars and thousands of people. At least in here, he could pretend he was in the country, enjoying the crisp air.

He'd told his guys he was going to start at the sixth green, which was at the back of the course itself. At only nine holes, the course was pretty easy to maintain. He'd start at six and work his way back to the storage shed. Hell, the grass didn't really need much mowing, not at this time of year. They could be done with a couple of hours to spare. He had some beers hidden in the back of the fridge in the shed. He and Willie and Sam could knock a few back while they waited to punch out.

With the mower rumbling beneath him and his headphones on, he couldn't hear the subway cars thumping down the raised tracks and that was just fine by him. His apartment would never make the cover of *Better Apartments and Gardens*. Noise and bad smells leaking in from the hallways, loud TVs and radios, fighting and the constant threat of crime were his constant companions at home.

Out here, he could pretend he was in the fields of Kentucky or West Virginia, where he'd lived for one year when he was young, working on a road project.

While he drove the mower, he sang an old BB King tune at the top of his voice. There was no one around to hear him, including himself. He knew he had a voice made for laryngitis, but sometimes, it felt good to belt out a song.

He drove along the green on a fixed pattern he could navigate in his sleep. While he mowed and sang, he daydreamed about those cold beers in the fridge.

Making a turn to mow around the putting green, Jefferson thought he saw a shadow to his left.

Goddamn kids. How many times do I have to chase them outta here? To make things worse, it was Halloween night, which was a built-in excuse for every mental midget in the neighborhood to climb the fence and ruin his perfect night.

Jefferson didn't mind it so much when they'd pop in to do a little horizontal loving in the sand pits. That was pretty harmless, and he didn't mind watching every now and then.

It was the ones who were up to no good, drinking and smoking dope or worse, that got his blood boiling. The last thing he wanted to do tonight was call the cops. But he'd heard about something going down at the cemetery just across the street earlier in the day. Had the news said people had died? He hadn't caught the whole report because he was too distracted spraying for roaches under his kitchen sink.

Pulling up the cutting blades, he turned the cart around to where he'd seen the shadowy figure.

It was still there, stumbling around, palely lit by the moonlight.

Whipping off his headphones, he muttered, "Stupid crack heads."

He drove straight for the doper, hoping to scare him off. Of course, if his head was up where the planes fly, the crack head might not even be aware Jefferson was heading for him.

The closer Jefferson got to the interloper, the larger the guy seemed. He wasn't just tall. He was about as wide as a shit house. Jefferson met Shaquille O'Neil outside Madison Square Garden after a game once and thought he was just about the biggest man he ever had or ever would see.

This tweaker made Shaq look like that funny guy, Kevin Hart.

Maybe he should call Willie and Sam for backup.

The shambling man finally stopped and turned Jefferson's way. Well, at least he had his attention.

"Get the hell out the golf course!" Jefferson shouted over the mover, waving his arm. Maybe the hulking guy would get the point and shuffle the hell on out of there.

Instead, the man said something. Or was it more like he made a crazy barking noise? Jefferson couldn't tell over the grating of the mower engine.

He pulled a little closer.

The man suddenly turned and started running at him!

"Oh shit!"

Jefferson cut the wheel to get out of the way.

The man got close enough to be captured by the light on the mower. Jefferson just about messed himself.

What the hell is it?

Hair covered everything but its face. And that face! It looked crazed. Its eyes were enormous black marbles set above a snapping mouth filled with some deadly looking teeth.

Jefferson had the cart in a ninety-degree turn but it wasn't enough. The man or monster slammed into the riding mower with the force of a train.

"Son of a biscuit!"

The mower was lifted off the ground. Jefferson saw it was about to roll over on top of him and leaped from his seat, his shoulder taking the brunt of the impact as he rolled onto the fairway.

Much to his dismay, the mower was rolling as well, and about to squash him like one of his roach roommates under his boot.

He kept on rolling, knowing he wouldn't have time to stop, get to his feet and haul ass. With each rotation, he saw the mower coming closer.

Why wasn't it stopping?

He got the answer on the next go around. The monster was running along with it, pushing the mower with what appeared to be reckless glee.

Jefferson rolled as fast as he could, shifting his momentum enough to where he hoped he was moving out of the way of the runaway mower.

"What the hell's going on?"

It was Sam.

Jefferson tumbled into a sand trap a hair before the mower would have crushed his legs. Because he'd been screaming for his life, he ended up with a mouth full of sand that he knew from experience was basically a litter box for the dozens of feral cats that lived around the course.

His arms and legs shook as he pushed himself up, spitting vile sand. He looked up in time to see Sam running like the calendar had been rolled back twenty years and he was a thirty-year old man with plenty of gas left in the tank.

The monster ran after Sam, but started zigging and zagging like a drunk trying to make it from the bar to his car. It stepped on its own feet and hit the turf hard enough for Jefferson to feel the impact seventy yards away.

Sam ran until he was out of sight. Jefferson tried to catch his breath. He ducked behind the crest of the sand trap, watching the massive creature as it got back unsteadily on its feet and proceeded to walk across the fairway as if nothing had happened.

Jefferson didn't know whether he should call the police or the zoo. When his boss saw the state of the mower, his ass was going to be in a sling. No way Mr. Farkle would believe it had been wrecked by a giant, hairy monster.

It took him a long while to get his jittery fingers to dial Willie's number.

"Willie. Stop what you're doing and meet me at the shed."

Those beers in the shed went from a want to a need. While Jefferson walked cautiously across the golf course, he kept trying to dial Sam, but his co-worker wasn't picking up the phone.

If he was smart, he'd keep on running until he found an open bar.

CHAPTER SIXTEEN

"What's wrong with you tonight?" Danielle asked as they walked to the next house. Meredith and Caitlin sprinted up the steps to Mrs. Lancomb's door. She'd been their first grade teacher and was a lovely older woman who had retired just the year before. Meredith was dressed as Jason from Friday the 13th. Vito much preferred that to the woodland fairy costume she'd originally wanted, being too naïve to realize it was more lingerie than a costume. But it had glitter and was multi-colored, which was enough to catch her eye.

"What?" Vito said, watching his daughter. "Nothing. I'm just enjoying being out with my girls." He hugged Danielle and kissed her cheek.

"I don't know. You and Shay are up to something."

Shay and Katie were talking to someone she knew at the hospital the next house down. Shay stole a quick glance at Vito that Danielle latched onto.

"You better not be planning to ditch us to go to a bar or something. You had your fun last night."

I wouldn't use the word fun to describe last night or today, Vito thought. "I wouldn't miss this for anything." He hugged her again. "I'm just a little tired. It was a long night."

She jabbed him in the stomach with a long-nailed finger. "You're getting old, buddy. Can't handle your liquor like you used to."

Vito gratefully accepted the excuse. "We're the same age, so you might want to think twice before mocking me."

Danielle playfully slapped his shoulder.

"Look what we got!" Meredith said, flashing a one pound chocolate bar.

"Wow. Did you thank Mr. Lancomb?" Danielle said.

Meredith and Caitlin's shoulders sagged. "Yes."

Danielle and Katie had been asking them that question at every house the past hour. Caitlin wore a zombie nurse costume smeared with fake blood as a semi-tribute to her mother. Vito had no idea when the girls had gotten into horror. They must have been watching that stuff on their phones. He hoped they weren't looking at the *other stuff* that was all too prevalent.

"Sweet score," Shay said, plucking the bar from his daughter's hand.

"Hey, give it back!"

Caitlin jumped as high as she could, reaching for the chocolate.

"Only if I can have a piece later," Shay joked.

Caitlin considered it for a moment and said, "Fine."

He handed it back to her and she joined Meredith at the gate to the next house.

"It's pretty light this year," Katie said, rejoining the group.

She was right. Normally by this point in the night, the streets were bustling with costumed kids. There were maybe half the usual out tonight. Many of the houses were decked out with decorations and orange lights, eagerly awaiting the masses that wouldn't be coming.

"Must be freaked out by all the weird stuff that happened today," Danielle said.

"I can't believe the playground is destroyed," Katie said. "Who would do such a thing?"

Last time Vito checked, the news was still saying it was the work of vandals. He was pretty damn sure the police were up to their assholes in reports about an animal being responsible for the carnage. For now, they were smart enough to keep it under wraps.

"And those murders at the cemetery," Danielle continued. Just hearing about it again gave Vito agita. "I'll bet it was the same group of people."

Katie's radar went up. "What makes you think it was a group of people?"

"You didn't see the playground? I'll show you tomorrow. No one person could do that. Or crash a funeral and murder four people without being taken down. Half those bagpipers were retired cops. Had to be the same group. I'll bet they're terrorists."

Vito had to stop that line of thinking. It could get out of control easily with Danielle. "Why would terrorists assault people at a funeral and wreck a playground? That doesn't make sense."

Yeah, as if a bigfoot doing it is just another slice of normal.

"Hello? To terrorize people. Look around you. There are a lot of upset kids that aren't out tonight because of it."

"The war against Halloween and its first world excesses," Shay said to lighten the mood.

"You're such an ass," Katie said to him.

"I fight terror with humor. Wins every time."

She leaned close to Shay and Vito overheard her whisper, "By the way, I'm still waiting for this big surprise I had to take a day off for."

Shay's eyes darted but he was quick to recover. "Patience, lady. Halloween's not over yet."

Vito wished he could joke around, but thinking about those four dead bagpipers weighed mightily on him.

At the next house, Katie and Danielle's friend Allison was standing at the door dressed as a devil or a hooker or a satanic hooker. Vito couldn't tell. She had twin sons around Meredith and Caitlin's age.

"You wanna come in for a glass of wine?" Allison asked.

"Don't mind if I do," Danielle said, grabbing Katie's hand. She turned to the girls. "You can hang out with Tim and Jimmy." The girls ran ahead of their moms. For the first time, Vito wondered if they had crushes on the boys. One more thing to worry about.

"You coming?" Katie said, stopping at the threshold while Danielle followed Allison inside. The sounds of some horror movie being played on the TV bled into the night.

"In there with the women and kids?" Shay said. Allison was divorced and got disturbingly frisky when she was drunk. "No thanks. Good time for a smoke break."

"We won't be long," Katie said, giving him a little finger wave before closing the door.

"Yes they will," Vito said.

Shay lit a cigarette and pulled out his phone, furiously tapping and swiping.

"You see anything?" Vito asked nervously. Tradition called for them all going back to his house when the trick or treating was over for Danielle's homemade lasagna. He didn't think he'd be able to eat one bite, and that would raise his wife's suspicions more than anything.

"Did you know that Britney Spears is staging a huge comeback world tour?" Shay said.

"You're an idiot."

"So far, so good. Maybe it's hibernating like a bear."

"There aren't any freaking caves to hide in in Van Cortlandt Park, so I don't think it's going to be able to hibernate for long."

A gaggle of kids, parents yapping in tow, walked past them, their excitement coming off them in waves. Vito wished he could snatch some of that and infuse it into his soul.

Shay leaned against a minivan and took a last drag on the cigarette before flicking it into the street. "Wait, this might be something."

"Crap. What?"

Shay turned his phone around to show him a picture of a smashed in gate. It looked like a truck had driven through it.

Vito studied every inch of the photo but couldn't see how it connected to their rogue bigfoot. "Yeah, so?"

"That was just posted on Instagram." He scrolled a bit so the caption underneath was visible. "The guy who took it says a bigfoot knocked the fence down at the Mosholu Golf Course."

Vito's heartbeat quickened. "How did you even find it?"

"I just put in a few bigfoot hashtags in the search. You're really not good with this stuff, are you?"

Vito had lost his virginity at the golf course. If he recalled correctly, it was on the eighth green.

Vito looked closer at the picture. "The question is, was it breaking in, or out of the golf course?"

Shay lit another cigarette. "I golfed there a few times with Plunkett. To me, that looks like part of the fence that leads to Jerome Avenue."

Shaking his head so hard his neck hurt, Vito said, "No way. There is no way some creature from the woods is going to wander under the L."

"It's getting a lot of likes. I think we should check it out."

"They'll kill us. Danielle already thinks we've got secret plans to go to the bar."

"Before her lasagna? No way!"

"Be serious."

Shay tucked the phone in his back pocket. "I am. We'll incur their wrath later. You told me this thing needs to be protected. You had a connection to it that I didn't, but I trust you. We can check it out and be back if nothing's happening before they finish their second glass of wine."

Vito could just imagine the blowback that would be heading his way. But Shay was right, which didn't happen often. He said, "Let's check it out."

They ran back to Vito's truck and were on the road heading for the raised subway and God knows what else.

In the Bronx, the subways were not always underground. They ran on elevated tracks that everyone called the L.

The bigfoot had no idea what an L or a train was, but when one of them clanked and sparked overhead, it ran for cover into a bus stop shelter. It also didn't know what glass was, so it crashed through the side of the enclosure, peppering the two women sitting on the bench with crumbles of safety glass. They screeched like a pair of bats and fled, leaving their pocketbooks behind, nearly getting clipped by a passing car.

Cowering under the broken shelter, the bigfoot assumed the train was the rumble of an oncoming storm. Its reaction was made all the more intense by the cocktail of drugs still coursing through a system that had never even experienced an aspirin. It stared up at the rising, rusted L pillars and the great tracks above. When a spray of sparks showered down, it shut its eyes and turned away. Once, when it had been much younger, a lightning strike that hit a tree thirty feet away had raised all of its hairs and sent it sprawling. It had been terrified of the light from the sky ever since.

As quickly as it came, it was over.

Several people gathered across the street, worriedly watching the large man in the gorilla costume. Some snapped pictures. Others warned them to steer clear. The man was obviously on something and could hurt them.

All the bigfoot saw was a group of big things that it feared almost as much as the sky fire.

Feeling that it was safe to step outside the shelter, it walked down Jerome Avenue, flinching at the sounds of cars and people as well as music that floated from the open door of the discount electronics store – that also did a robust trade on burner phones – on the other side of the road. The cacophony of noises would have sent it running faster than the mechanical sasquatch in the old *Bionic Man* TV show, but for now, all the bigfoot could do was plod onward, trying to reconcile what it was seeing and hearing through a very distorted lens with what it had always known and now craved.

The sidewalk still felt unseemly under its feet, but it was no longer repulsed. It kept to the shadows on the sidewalk. To its right was a long running fence, another playground (though this one dark and mercifully vacant) and trees behind the fence.

Across the two-way road that ran under the L was block after block of stores and bars. The sasquatch looked at the garish light of a yellow Western Union sign and blinked hard, the luminous glow stabbing its eyes. This was not the bright yellow in the day sky, but it was just as painful to glimpse full on.

When a car sped by, beeping its horn, the bigfoot leaped to its right, hit into the fence and staggered for a moment. So many moving shiny things. They were everywhere. Even more of them were still, lined one after the other. The bigfoot felt they were watching and waiting. It feared them more than the ones that sped up and down the path.

Filled with piteous terror, the bigfoot tilted its head back and cried a wail that brought the noises of the city to its knees.

Every man, woman and child within earshot stopped what they were doing and looked for what could possibly make such a sound. To many, they mistook it for the dying wail of one of the old L pillars. They ran from the area, not wanting to be near when the tracks collapsed on top of them, the ignorant policies of the no-good mayor claiming yet more lives.

A young couple and their small children, all dressed for Halloween, who happened to be walking toward the bigfoot, screamed with equal terror, turned around and ran down the street. This brought the bigfoot out of its pity party, alarmed that they had been so close.

Without thinking of where it was going, it ran toward the street, hurtling over a parked car. The top of the antenna whacked its shin. It was just enough of a distraction for the sasquatch to turn the wrong way and land awkwardly on the blacktop.

Its timing was as poor as its luck.

A teen driving his father's Toyota Corolla who had been preoccupied texting his girlfriend never saw the hairy creature drop onto the road. He didn't even have time to stomp on the brakes.

The front of the Toyota crumpled as if it were made of origami as it struck the bigfoot's massive thighs. The airbag deployed, slamming the driver's hand and the phone into his face, breaking his nose.

Outside of the wreck, the bigfoot flipped over the car. When it landed on its back on the trunk, the back half of the car crumpled.

An SUV driving too close behind the Toyota skidded straight ahead, slamming the demolished car. The bigfoot was catapulted back over the car, tumbling end over end and down the road. Fur and blood painted the double yellow line as it continued its uncontrolled roll into oblivion.

CHAPTER SEVENTEEN

Diego was pissed. Some motherfucker in a monkey suit gets his ass splattered and now the whole place was going to be crawling with pigs. He leaned against one of the L pillars, shooting daggers at the mound of fur and blood.

"What's the matter, papi?" he shouted. "You deserve to get your shit pushed in, pendejo!"

He should have known things were too good to be true. The Halloween hustle had been going gangbusters. He'd sold almost half the molly he'd started with and was looking forward to going back to his crib early and watching *Saw* movies, smoking and drinking until he passed out. Now this freak went and blew up his spot.

The cars that had hit the sucker were in pretty bad shape. The drivers may have been even worse. Neither was moving behind their respective wheels. There was a lot of blood inside the windshield of the Toyota. Motherfuckers were jacked the hell up.

Nobody gave a shit about nothing in this hood except when tragedy struck. Then every asshole had to drop what they were doing to ogle. Things were getting crowded real fast. Traffic was stopped in both directions. Lots of phones were out taking video and pictures of the wreck and especially gorilla dude.

Five failed court ordered stints at anger management had done little to soften Diego's edges. When he got mad, he went from mildly disturbed to furious faster than a Ferrari on the Autobahn.

He should be walking away and searching for another prime place to peddle his shit.

He should assume the dude who had ruined his night was dead and leave it at that.

But damn, he was flaming hot angry.

Everyone kept their distance from the body. Some tried to wake the people up in the cars.

Before Diego could stop himself, he slid out from his hiding place and stormed over to the costumed cunt.

Keeping his back to the people who had their phones out, he squatted near the guy's face. It was a real nice costume – totally realistic shit. He'd give him that. That and something else.

Diego kicked the guy square in the chest. His toes blazed with instant agony. The body didn't even move an inch.

Several people gasped, while someone in the crowd blurted, "Yeah, fuck him up!"

That made Diego smile, egging him on.

He kicked again, this time in the dude's stomach, expecting it to be softer, more forgiving.

Man, was he wrong.

Was he wearing some kind of steel-enforced costume? It would explain how those cars got to be totaled like that.

One thing he was sure of, the bastard was dead.

That didn't stop Diego.

"That's what you get for coming into my hood."

He culled up something wet and gelatinous from deep in his lungs and spat on the man's dark skinned face.

"Fuck up my night. Bye, bye, bitch."

The sound of incoming sirens was his cue to get out. He'd hop the fence and cut across the park and come out around the Mosholu Parkway. He had a couple of spots over that way that might do him good.

Diego stepped over the body but was stopped midway. He looked down and couldn't believe his eyes.

The guy was alive and had an iron grip on his ankle.

Diego tried to tug his leg free. "Get offa me, cabron!"

The fingers, which were twice the size of any fingers he'd ever seen, squeezed hard enough to make him lose feeling in his foot. Unbalanced, Diego fell onto his chest. His plastic baggie of pills shot out of his jacket pocket and skittered across the street, settling underneath a parked car.

His fury inflamed to phoenix level. No one messed with his drugs. That was his livelihood.

Rolling onto his back, he struck out with his free foot, nailing the guy's side. Instead of getting him to loosen his grip, it only spurred him into sitting up, then getting to his feet, lifting Diego off the ground as he stood.

"Put me down, asshole!"

Diego dangled upside down, helpless as a newborn fresh from the birth canal.

What sounded like the same voice from before said, "Fuck him up, bro!" Only this time, Diego wasn't sure who he was urging on.

His knife! It was in his back pocket. If he could reach it, he'd teach this nut a lesson.

Swaying slightly, he reached behind him, his fingers grazing his pocket.

Damn, this guy was strong, especially for someone who just got creamed by two cars. And big as hell, unless he was wearing some kind of platform boots or something.

The tip of his index finger brushed against the cold steel of his switchblade. He knew switchblades were terrible for defense, but they looked cool and scared off people he didn't want near him most times.

The sirens were getting closer. He needed to get his ass clear of this psycho.

Managing to ease the switchblade toward his thumb, he pinched it free and moved it to his palm where he easily hit the trigger to release the blade. He jabbed the dude right in the arm and laughed. "I told you to let me down."

A blood curdling roar erupted from the man's throat. The pressure on Diego's ankle doubled…tripled…until he heard and felt his ankle bones snap.

Diego cried out for someone to help him.

No one moved.

But they sure didn't drop their phones.

Next thing he knew, he was being lifted up and swung in the air like he was a lasso. Pleading for mercy, his stomach about to give up the Popeye's he'd had for lunch, he saw the L pillar coming at his face a split second before his skull broke apart like cherry flavored rock candy thrown against a wall.

Shay knew they had found their bigfoot when Vito stopped at the light just before entering under the L on Jerome Avenue. Just a few feet ahead, cars were at a dead stop. The people running down the street and sidewalk, some casting worried glances backward, told him all he needed to know.

"Could be a shooting or robbery," Vito said, as if this would ease their minds. Gunplay and theft were familiar to them. Any Bronx denizen took that in stride.

Shay rolled his window down. A woman old enough to be his grandmother must have found Jesus, because she was running like a teen, shouting, "Monster! Monster!" at the top of her lungs.

He looked over at Vito. "You were saying."

"We'll have to hoof it. No way I can get through this traffic."

Vito backed the truck up and pulled into a rare empty space by the curb. When they got out of the truck, he slapped his head hard enough to make Shay wince. "Fuck. I forgot our rifles."

"Two white guys with rifles traipsing down Jerome Avenue would not be a good look. Plenty of people have guns. Remember, our job is to wave the flag for peace and love and bigfoot acceptance."

Trudging toward the elevated subway, Vito grumbled, "Yeah, I know. I'd just feel safer with a gun, you know, in case something goes wrong."

Walking right beside him, Shay said, "You mean to tell me things have been going right so far?"

"You know what I'm talking about, dummy."

Unfortunately, Shay did. Here they were coming to try to save the bigfoot and they could end up just like that deer back in the park. Or Shay's crappy shed. Or the bagpipers in the cemetery. Could a sasquatch differentiate between friend and foe? They were about to find out without any means of self-defense.

I should have told Katie and Caitlin I love them.

Then again, that would have roused his wife's suspicion and they might not have been able to steal themselves away.

And that's a bad thing? Shay thought.

They had to go several blocks before they came across the cringeworthy car wreck. The night pulsed with red and white strobes of light. Ambulance crews and cops tended to the people still trapped in their smashed vehicles. Other cops were keeping the growing flock of ghouls at bay. From what Shay could tell, most of the initial witnesses had fled. The new influx of lookie-loos came streaming from side streets, attracted by the sights and sounds of chaos.

"Why is everybody getting so cranked up about a car accident?" Vito said, staring at the grievously wounded person behind the wheel in the SUV.

Shay's eyes had wandered elsewhere and quickly discovered why the old lady had been screeching about a monster.

Lying in a twisted heap of broken limbs was a headless body. The splat zone of what he assumed was the person's head started on one of the L pillars and fanned out in a fifteen-foot radius. The doors and windows of parked cars next to it looked as if they'd been strafed by soft tomatoes.

"You might want to check this out," Shay said to his friend.

Vito turned his head and immediately spun away. "You could have warned me."

"Come on. I know you've seen some twisted shit in your job. What about that homeless guy who froze to the park bench?"

"He just looked like he was sleeping. It wasn't like he was a frozen can of soda in the back of the fridge that exploded."

The wind shifted and the overpowering odor of copper and the inside bits of a person that should never be smelled crept up Shay's nose. "Okay, I'm ready to move along now. Only question is, which way did it go?"

Vito motioned toward two teens being interviewed by a police officer. They were pointing down the street, talking animatedly, though a passing train blocked out what they were saying.

"Looks like it's heading toward Gun Hill Road," Shay said.

"Remember when we used to ride our bikes there in the summer to buy sugar cane from that street vendor we couldn't understand?"

"Nothing better than chewing on that sugar cane."

They started walking.

"I wish we were back in time right about now." Vito kept stealing glances at the fenced-in little park to their right.

Shay stopped to look at the hood of a car that had what looked like the imprint of a fist dented in the Detroit steel. Stepping closer to the car, he caught the lingering aroma of the beast.

"Fuck me," Vito said behind him. "Can you imagine what'll happen to us if we get punched like that?"

Shay took out his phone and turned on the flashlight to get a better look. The paint was smeared with blood and there were a few hairs left behind. No doubt about what had taken its anger out on the vehicle.

"I'm going to choose not to," Shay said. "Katie says I'm hard headed, but not harder than steel."

A choir of screams up ahead sent a shiver down his back.

Why can't I just ignore it all and go home?

One look at Vito told him his buddy was having the same thoughts. But then he turned to see where the headless body had been and knew his guilt for bringing this destructive force of nature to the neighborhood would never let him sit this out.

With a deep sigh, he lit up another cigarette and resumed walking. "Duty calls."

It wasn't long before they were fighting their way through a tide of terrified humanity. The glass of a stationery storefront had been smashed in. A light pole was on the ground, sparks spitting out of its broken end. A man was on the ground, a human welcome mat that was missed by very few scuttling feet.

Complete and utter pandemonium.

With the smell getting worse, they knew they were getting closer.

Shay would give anything to be fourteen again, balancing long reeds of sugar cane on his handlebars as he pedaled his bike back home, mouth watering at the thought of what was to come.

No sweet rewards tonight.
At best, he figured, it would be just desserts.

CHAPTER EIGHTEEN

The bigfoot had never been utterly engulfed by this many creatures before. The big and small things made such strange, irritating noises, running into him in some cases. Their touch made the sasquatch recoil and sometimes lash out.

With the drugs not finished with their handiwork, the bigfoot was in a state of perplexity, unsure if what it was seeing and hearing was real or part of the nothing time when it settled down to sleep. It felt very real, but so had many of the nothing time visions.

Staggering against the unruly mob, it grabbed ahold of a man who had the audacity to run blindly into its chest.

"No! Please! No!" the man blubbered.

Without a glimmer of understanding what the man spoke, the bigfoot tossed him aside and through the plate glass window of Raj's Newsstand. Raj, the owner, had been busy playing a game with his headphones on, oblivious to what was going on outside. When the body and shattered glass swarmed over him, he tossed his phone aside, ready to use the bat he had under his counter on the thug who had destroyed his window.

Flicking glass off his shoulder, he grabbed the bat, a Louisville Slugger he'd gotten at Yankee Stadium bat day, and jumped through the empty window frame. People were running everywhere. What the hell was going on?

When he saw the giant man in the gorilla costume, he knew he'd spotted the source of the melee.

"Did you do this to my store?" he demanded.

The man turned to him, his near-black eyes glassy and dazed. Wow, that was one hell of a realistic costume.

Raj shook the thought away. No matter what, this costumed crazy had wrecked his storefront.

"You son of a bitch!" Raj snarled, whacking the man in the upper arm with the bat.

The Yankee Stadium relic broke in half.

The man snarled at him and Raj knew, looking into that horrific open maw, that this was no costume. His bowels went south in a hurry and he tried to backpedal into his store. If he could get to the basement door, maybe this…this thing would move on and not break him like the bat.

The creature lashed out and latched onto his face. It felt as if his skull were going to be crushed until it was a fine powder. It slammed Raj onto the ground. Raj went from scared senseless and wrapped in the folds of agony to insensate in an instant.

As the bigfoot moved on and more people tried to escape its path, dozens of feet stomped on Raj's unmoving back.

A wave of dizziness sent the bigfoot staggering sideways. It reached out to grab anything to keep it on its feet. When its fingers came in contact with the icy metal of a streetlight, it reacted with disgust, tearing the light from the ground. It bounced hard, nearly taking the legs out of a trio of senior citizens who were doing their best to haul ass out of the way.

Something hard hit the bigfoot in the back. It spun around, nearly losing its equilibrium, temper flaring as it searched for what had hit it.

A red brick, now in pieces, lay on the sidewalk.

Two pre-teen boys ran like the wind, satisfied that they had at least tried to take down the crazed animal.

The sasquatch scooped up the pieces of brick and threw them at the stores, breaking more windows. Shards of glass stuck in the skin of the fleeing populace. A woman wailed that she couldn't see. Her hands covered her eyes, blood seeping from between her fingers.

Its mind reeling, the bigfoot roared at the large things around it, wanting them to go far away, to leave it be.

A snarling dog caught its attention. A man dressed as a skeleton leaned back against the taut leash. Slather dripped from the pit bull's mouth. It had been a rescue dog and had taken the better part of a year to retrain. Originally owned by a drug dealer, it had been raised to kill on command. The scent of the wild animal was driving it insane.

"No, Petey, no!" its owner said. He tried desperately to rein the dog in. He was supposed to take his niece out trick or treating but first had to walk the dog. It was a sure bet that trick or treating was done for the night after this. All he wanted to do now was get Petey to come to his senses so they could both get their asses home. No matter how hard he tried, he was no match for the pit bull.

The leash slipped from his fingers with a final, brutal tug.

"Petey!"

The pit bull charged the sasquatch like a bullet train. Its inbred penchant for violence had come to the fore and it needed to feel its iron jaws clamped down on the flesh of the animal before it.

If it hadn't been drugged, the bigfoot would have easily dodged the crazed dog. Unfortunately, it could only watch in mild wonder as the dog leaped and latched onto its wrist. Never before had an animal in its home ever dared to attack it. The new experience made the bigfoot even slower to react.

But then the pain hit.

It yowled in agony, swinging its arm in a desperate attempt to shake the dog free. The pit bull only chomped down harder.

The bigfoot spun in a wild circle, whimpering now because it felt as if the dog's teeth were going to break right through its bones. It slammed the dog into a wall, eliciting a slight whimper, but failing to lessen the pain.

Running in agony and confusion, the bigfoot's granite hips checked into the fleeing crowd, scattering people like a hurricane through an amusement park. It turned the corner, leaving the busy street behind it, skirting along high rise apartment buildings. The pit bull refused to let go.

Realizing that running wasn't helping, the bigfoot stopped, raised its arm and looked the dog in the eyes. It saw nothing there but raw blood lust.

Squealing tires and the smell of burnt rubber filled the air as drivers spotted the bizarre struggle between beast and monster.

Drawing its free hand back, the bigfoot slapped the dog on the side of its head, setting one of its eyeballs free from its socket.

The dog's mouth opened wide as it yelped.

The bigfoot went to stomp its head to make it pay for the pain it had inflicted.

But the pit bull wasn't finished. Even wounded, it still wanted to fight. It dove for the bigfoot's thigh, clamping down on foul smelling hair and muscle.

This pain was worse than before.

Reaching down with both meaty hands, the bigfoot grabbed the dog by its sides and pulled it free, along with a hunk of its own flesh. In one sweeping motion, it flung the dog high and wide, sending it sailing across the street packed with stopped cars, over the fence and into the park.

The dog rolled for ten feet before popping back up. It charged the fence, its senses latched onto the scent of the bigfoot and wanting to finish what it started. It snarled and barked, but it couldn't clear the fence.

People had gotten out of their cars to get a better look at the bigfoot. No one quite understood what they were seeing. Was it a man or some kind of escaped animal? When it moved out of the oval of illumination from the overhead streetlights, it was possible to mistake it for a bear. How the hell did a bear get loose in the Bronx?

Actually, anything was possible in the New York borough. Some idiot probably thought having a bear for a pet would be cool, at least until it grew too big to hide away, feed and control.

Horns honked and people shouted.

The bigfoot did not like the sound of the honking horns in the slightest. Its leg and wrist throbbed. All it wanted to do was find a shadow to slink into and hide.

As tired and bedraggled as it was, it was once again on the run, seeking any kind of sanctuary.

Shay and Vito made it through the panicked crowd a little worse for wear. There would be bruises tomorrow, that was for sure.

When Shay saw the snarl of cars on West Gun Hill Road, he knew they were on the right track. A pit bull behind the park fence barked until he was sure its throat would spit blood. When it moved into the light, seeking a way through the fence, he got a good look at its face and shivered.

"Vito, look at that!"

Blood and viscera dripped from its vacant eye socket. That was a very fresh wound.

"Don't think I'd be up to much if that was me," Shay said, astonished by the animation in the dog.

"You get too close to that fence and it *will* be you." Vito grabbed Shay's arm, hard. "Check it out!"

The sidewalk was stained with blood spatter. A hunk of something wet and hairy was right next to Shay's foot. He touched it with his toe and jumped back. It quivered as it turned over, revealing pink and gray flesh. "What the fuck is that?"

Vito got down on one knee to get closer, but only for a moment. He quickly shot back up and pinched his nose. "That's a piece of the bigfoot."

Shay looked back over at the snarling dog. "You think?"

Nodding, Vito said, "You want to put your nose to it to confirm? We're close."

"Believe it or not, that's not very comforting."

At least the sasquatch had left them a trail they couldn't miss. Shay would have thanked the pit bull, but he liked his limbs attached.

They followed the droplets of blood down the sidewalk of West Gun Hill Road. Shay recalled reading that there had been a gang shootout in this area three weeks ago between rival Puerto Rican and Dominican gangs. The neighborhood had been home to the disparate groups for as long as he could remember. A few shots fired were nothing new.

A bigfoot wandering the neighborhood, now that was worthy of a headline.

They noticed that the blood was close to the apartment buildings. Up ahead, they heard the high-pitched screeches of small children. Without worry for his own safety, Shay ran with Vito hot on his heels.

CHAPTER NINETEEN

The bigfoot saw a group of the small things up ahead, coming its way. But something was different. They didn't look at all like any of the small things it had seen before. They smelled and sounded the same, but their appearance had it on even higher alert. There was no place to hide and the shadows were too thin.

Its nervous eyes rolled to its left and right.

The creature that had bitten it followed it from across the path, snarling and unafraid.

The sasquatch's leg and wrist were pounding. Its hands hurt from hitting things. Its head was starting to clear, but the countenance of the small ones made it feel as if it were still in the grips of a dizzying delusion.

Behind it, the bigfoot heard the raucous chaos of too many big things and other alien sounds. Plus, there was the screaming. So much screaming in this place that was not home. It had never encountered anything like it. Home on its loudest stormy night was nothing but a whisper compared to this.

The small things came closer. Their laughter should have calmed the sasquatch.

Now, it just wanted to flee, but it didn't know where it could go.

Terrified as it was, the bigfoot rose to its full height to show its strength and strode forward.

The first child to notice it was a nine-year old girl named Courtney dressed as a witch. She wore a rubber mask that had a long, pointed nose with a wart on the end. She'd looped the handle of her goodie bag over her broom, the long handle resting on her shoulder so she resembled a gruesome tramp with her bindle. Her older brother by three years kept threatening to steal the juice box she'd gotten at one of the apartments in the last building they'd gone into. Tony wore a Scream mask and carried a huge, fake knife.

"Oh wow, look at that bigfoot costume!" she said excitedly, pointing at the approaching creature.

"Whoa," her friend Martika said. "It looks so real." Martika was festooned in a Pokémon costume her grandmother had made her that looked way better than anything she could find in a store. Gramma Tyson used to work as a seamstress for some designer back in the day.

"Damn, he's huge. I wonder if he's walking on stilts," Tony said.

His friend Craig waved at the air. "What's that smell?"

Martika pinched her nose and replied in a nasally twang, "I think it's garbage."

"Or maybe the sewer," Courtney said. She couldn't take her eyes off the bigfoot costume. Her father had bought her a Blu-ray of *Harry and the Hendersons* for her fifth birthday and she had watched it more times than she could count. That Christmas, she had told her parents that she was going to ask Santa for a pet bigfoot. They had explained that a bigfoot would be too big and heavy for Santa's sleigh. She'd gotten a betta fish instead.

When the fake bigfoot was just ten feet away, she called out to him. "Hey mister, that's the best bigfoot costume ever."

She wanted to ask him if he liked *Harry and the Hendersons*, too, but the smell got even worse and she had to clamp her mouth shut. No amount of candy could cut through the horrid taste in the air.

"Check it out, he even made it so it looks like it's hurt," Craig said, pointing out the raw, red and bloody hunk in its leg.

"It's even dripping," Tony said.

They stopped to let the man pass, marveling at the sheer amount of work that went into the costume. Courtney bet he made it by himself. She'd seen videos of people who went to costume conventions and was amazed by what they could create.

But this, this was beyond special.

The man in the bigfoot suit cast a cursory glance down at them but kept walking.

Until Courtney reached out to touch him.

She wanted to see what the fur felt like, even though she wanted to puke from that weird smell. It felt like running her palm over a thorny bush.

"Ow!" she cried, pulling her hand back.

Her touch surprised the man, because he raised his arms and bared his teeth and made a growling noise that she felt in her bones as much as she heard.

It was at that moment they all realized this was no man in a costume.

It was a monster. A real freaking monster!

Treat bags were dropped. Candy spilled all over the sidewalk. The four children ran as if their lives depended on it, shedding their masks as they went.

The bigfoot ran in the opposite direction, turning a corner and coming face to face with dozens and dozens of similar small things out and about.

The sasquatch's heartbeat thrummed in its ears.

The screaming started again.

It turned and ran, heading back onto West Gun Hill Road.

As it passed by an apartment building, it spotted a dark stairwell. The bigfoot jumped down the stairs and crashed into a steel door. Eyes flicking to the top of the stairwell, it listened to the screams.

Suddenly, the door opened and the bigfoot tumbled through the doorway.

A voice said, "You didn't have to knock so loud, you know."

And then its legs were moved aside and the door was slammed shut.

The blood trail had gotten thinner and that put a pin in the hope balloon in Vito's head. Four terrified children bustled past him and Shay, yelling for their mommies.

He was tempted to stop one of them and ask them what they saw, but in this day and age, one who was a stranger did not talk to little kids, especially when it looked like he'd have to grab one to slow them down.

Vito and Shay hurried on, feeling that the bigfoot had to be just around the corner.

There were more scared kids on Decker Road and a few concerned adults. But behind them were the usual gaggle of trick or treaters.

"It definitely didn't go that way," Vito said. He was breathing heavier than he should, considering he did cardio at the gym four days a week.

The stress is going to give me a heart attack.

Here he was running headlong to intercept a bigfoot that might very well snap him in half. Maybe Shay was right. Maybe they should go home, watch the news and keep this awful secret to themselves.

"Let's try the next block," Shay said, pointing at a couple of droplets of blood on the ground illuminated by his phone's light.

Then Vito thought of the strange intelligence he'd seen in the bigfoot's eyes. It was hurt and obviously scared. If it wanted to just randomly slaughter people, it would have left a killing field in its wake. It lashed out for a reason. Vito was sure of it. Just because he didn't know the reason didn't change his stance that they should try to save it.

Would it know he and Shay were the ones who shanghaied it from its home? That would be reason enough to separate their heads from their necks.

They made it to Cox Road and didn't see anything strange or unusual.

"Looks like the bleeding stopped," Vito said, scanning the ground with his light.

Shay leaned over with his hands on his knees, panting. The last time he'd seen the interior of a gym was the last gym class they'd taken in high school almost twenty years ago. "Or it just disappeared."

"Something that big can't just disappear." Vito willed Shay's body to recover quicker. The longer they stayed here, the colder the trail got.

"There are theories out there that bigfoot is, what did they call it, *an inter-dimensional traveler* that sometimes gets lost between two worlds. Maybe it went back to where it belongs."

Vito shook his head. "It belongs upstate."

"A UFO could have scooped it up."

"Are you just fucking with me at this point, or have you truly lost your mind?"

Shay waved him off. "Fucking with you...I think. Or wishful thinking."

They walked around West Gun Hill Road for a bit, but all was calm and normal. The snarling, wounded dog in the park had disappeared. Kids hustled across streets with parents close behind, their treat bags bulging. Even the chaos on Jerome Avenue couldn't stop the holiday. The further they got from it, the more people they saw out and about. A couple of teen boys wearing all black rode past them on their bikes. They had a bag of raw eggs that they tossed at the buildings as they rode along, shouting, "Happy Halloween suckers!"

"Amateurs," Shay said, watching them pedal out of sight.

Vito remembered him and Shay running from the cops on a few Halloween nights, their pockets loaded with eggs and shaving cream.

"I say we circle back. It definitely didn't go this far," Vito said.

This was perplexing. How could a seven-foot bigfoot seemingly vanish into thin air? What Shay had said about it being inter-dimensional was a load of horseshit, but Vito was starting to have his doubts.

They were now at the Mosholu Parkway. The big rehab center was across the way. Traffic moved in a steady, no-bigfoot-has-passed-here flow.

Shay looked at his phone. "How many times has Danielle called you?"

Vito stuck his phone in his pocket. "I'm almost too afraid to look."

"No way am I listening to voicemail. We better tell them we're alive before they really kill us."

"And where do we tell them we are?"

"I need to think that one through. This is one case where the truth will not set us free."

They walked back, wondering now what was scarier: an angry bigfoot or a fuming wife.

CHAPTER TWENTY

Destiny Russell looked at the big, fuzzy animal lying on the floor and put her hands on her hips. She'd been playing with her My Little Pony dolls in the apartment building's basement when it had bashed on the door. At first she'd been startled, but then she thought maybe someone was frightened and needed to get inside. Her mother had told her about all the scary things that could happen outside and Destiny promised she would never go out alone.

Imagine her delight when it was not some person but a big, cuddly beast like in her favorite book, *Where the Wild Things Are*.

"How did you get off the island?" she asked it. "I'm not Max, but I can be your friend."

It leapt to its feet when she got too close. She was afraid it was going to go back out the door, but then its face screwed up in pain and it grabbed its leg with one of its hands. She saw the blood and knew it was hurt.

"Who did that to you?"

The beast stared at her but didn't respond. Of course not, it was a beast of the wild.

"We need to bandage you up," Destiny said. "Stay right there. I'll be back."

She headed across the room lined with steel cages, most of them filled with bikes and boxes and holiday decorations that belonged to the people who lived in her building. Coming to the laundry room that had two washing machines and three dryers, she opened one of the dryer drawers and found a warm, clean washcloth. "This'll do."

Destiny skipped back to her wounded beast and thrust her hand holding the cloth out. "Here, you can put it on your boo boo. It's clean. I swear."

The beast leaned forward and sniffed the washcloth. Destiny giggled.

"I like the way things smell when they come out of the dryer. Go on. Take it. It'll make you feel better."

When the beast didn't move, she knelt down and pressed the fabric to the open wound. The beast staggered back and the washcloth fell on the floor.

"Now you made it dirty. If I put it on now, you'll get an infection. Let me see if there's another one."

She headed back to the dryer, not concerned that Mrs. Nguyen would be very upset if she knew Destiny was taking her clean linens and giving them to a hurt beast.

The bigfoot watched her leave and its heart settled down.

The big thing seemed so much like a small thing, it didn't know what to do. There was no way it could know that even though Destiny Russell was nineteen years of age and a couple of inches shy of six feet, she had the innocence and mental capacity of a five-year old. The whole neighborhood loved Destiny and looked out for her. She was stunningly beautiful, which tended to attract a lot of undue attention when she was outside with her mother or aunts. The men in the area made it very clear to anyone leering her way that they had best keep on moving.

Destiny liked to play in the basement. Even though other people came down here to do their laundry or take things from their storage cages, it felt like her own little clubhouse. This was the first time a beast had ever come to play. She grabbed a yellow towel and gave it to her visitor. This time, the beast took the towel, though it didn't put it on its boo boo.

"What am I going to do with you?" She couldn't help herself from giggling. Any do-do would know you have to put something on a bad cut. But not this beast.

"Are you hungry?"

It just stared at her.

She reached into her pocket and took out a granola bar. They were some of her favorite snacks, after popcorn with lots of butter. The paper crinkled as she unwrapped it. The beast's eyes lit up when she took a bite and offered it the rest. This time it knew what to do. It slurped the bar down without so much as chewing.

"You'll get a stomach ache eating like that," she scolded the beast. It smacked its lips.

119

"I get thirsty when I eat them, too. I can share my water with you."

In her suitcase of My Little Ponies was a bottle of water. She unscrewed the cap, took a sip and held it out.

The beast took the water, but it squeezed the bottle too hard. Water splashed up into its face and it jumped so high, its head hit the ceiling. The bottle bounced on the floor.

Destiny bent over laughing. "Do that again!" She picked up the bottle and tried to give it back. The beast wouldn't touch it this time.

"You're funny. Want to play with me?" She sat on the floor and crossed her legs. She patted the cement floor. "Sit next to me. I'll let you play with Rainbow Dash, even though she's my favorite. I'll be Pinkie Pie."

The beast loomed over her until she grabbed its hand and practically pulled it down beside her. She was very strong, much stronger than she could ever realize. Destiny was always careful how she touched people. She never wanted to hurt anyone. But her beast, he was big and strong and she was sure it could handle a little tug.

"Here." She put Rainbow Dash in its hand.

The beast opened its mouth and tossed the plastic toy inside. It masticated on Rainbow Dash with a look of confusion on its dark face.

Destiny got extremely upset. The beast was ruining her toy!

"No, no, no! Don't eat it! You're wrecking it. Stop it! Spit it out right now!"

The bigfoot cowered at the big/small thing's command. It didn't know what it was telling him, but it knew territorial anger. It looked toward the door and was about to get up and run again when the tone of the big/small thing's voice changed.

"Don't leave. I'm sorry. I have another Rainbow Dash. Look. It's right here." Destiny pulled an identical toy from the bag. She let her beast see it for a moment and stashed it away. She didn't want it wrecking that one, too. Then she'd have none. "You must be really hungry to eat my pony. I wish I had more food to share with you, but my mom only lets me have one snack after dinner. Hey, I'm going trick or treating later. Do you wanna come with me?"

Destiny played with her ponies for a moment, talking out loud and doing her best to make them sound the way they did in the cartoons. She kept glancing at her beast, wondering if he was going to join in or not.

"There's something I want to tell you, but you're not supposed to say mean things about people."

The beast cocked its head, staring at her as if it wanted her to say it anyway.

"But, well, I guess since you're not people, it's okay." She took a deep breath and blurted out, "You smell really bad. Like really, really bad."

The beast didn't seem to mind.

Destiny pressed on. "I should name you Stinky, but that wouldn't be nice." Her eyes suddenly lit up and she jumped to her feet. "I know! I can make you smell a whole lot better. Follow me."

She started walking toward the laundry area and turned around. Her beast just sat there. Motioning with her hands, she urged it on. "Come on. I promise it's not anything scary."

It rose to its feet, its head just a few inches shy of scraping the ceiling. It slowly followed her, like the scaredy cats she sometimes fed at the park. Why were animals such chickens?

Destiny searched the shelves for the fabric softener with the teddy bear on it. That was one of her favorite smells in the world. It would be so easy if she could just put the beast in the washing machine.

She opened the plastic cap and tilted the bottle, pouring some of the thick, blue fluid into her palm. When her beast was close enough to touch, she applied some of the fabric softener to the hair on its arm. The beast yanked its arm away at first, but she laughed and called it a silly goose. "Don't be such a baby."

Next came the other arm, and then a little on its chest. Destiny was tall, but even she had a hard time getting some on the hair on the top of its head. She wished her beast could understand her when she told it to sit down. Oh well, at least it was starting to smell a little less yucky.

The sasquatch now dripped blue goo and looked like it had been partially crossed with a Smurf. This set Destiny to giggling once again.

"Sweet D, what are you up to?"

Mrs. Hobbes's voice came from somewhere behind the girl and monster.

"Sounds like you're having yourself a good…"

The elderly woman was Destiny's neighbor from across the hall. She dropped the plastic bin of dirty clothes she'd brought down to wash. "Who are you?" she said to the beast.

"Oh, hi Mrs. Hobbes. It's my beast. I haven't given him a name yet, though I was thinking of Stinky. Do you think that's too mean? Mom said I should never be mean."

Mrs. Hobbes burned the bigfoot with her concerned gaze. "I said who are you and what are you doing down here?"

"Why are you so angry?" Destiny asked.

"Sweet D, I need you to come to me."

"Why?"

"Because I said so, honey."

"Are you scared of Stinky? There's nothing to be scared of."

Mrs. Hobbes inched toward Destiny, her eyes locked on the bigfoot. "Did he do anything to you? You can tell Auntie Hobbes."

Destiny looked at her, confused. "He did try to eat my Rainbow Dash. But I think he's sorry. Right?" She looked up at her beast, who couldn't take its eyes off of Mrs. Hobbes. "I think you're making him scared."

"I sincerely doubt that, honey. Now, I want you to go upstairs and get your mother. Can you do that for me?"

Destiny toed the floor. "Will you keep Stinky company?"

Mrs. Hobbes breathed heavily. "Sure, Sweet D. Sure. Now go run along."

Destiny started to go but stopped. "What should I tell her?"

"Tell her to call the police."

"Police? Why? Is someone in trouble?"

The ebbing of Mrs. Hobbes's patience was visible on her face. "No more questions. Just do what I asked, okay?"

"The police scare me."

Mrs. Hobbes leaned forward as far as she could, her feet barely moving as she didn't want to get too close to the bigfoot, and grabbed Destiny's arm. "Go, now. Go!"

Destiny recoiled and shouted, "Ow. You hurt me!" Tears immediately sprang from her eyes.

Her beast saw this and puffed itself up so it seemed like it filled every corner of the basement. It stomped toward Mrs. Hobbes and belched a loud and long roar right in her face, dislodging the bun on the top of her head.

Now Mrs. Hobbes was crying, her glasses slipping off her nose and breaking on the floor. She turned around and ran as fast as her old legs would carry her, screaming every inch of the way.

"Wait! He didn't mean to scare you!" Destiny called after her. She turned to her beast. "You didn't, right?"

Her beast watched her neighbor slam through the door to the stairs.

"We have to tell her you're sorry. If she gets my mother upset, we'll both be in trouble."

Latching onto her beast's finger, she dragged it along as she chased after Mrs. Hobbes. The pair entered the stairway and heard the clatter of the woman's footsteps above them, followed by the tapping of her shoes on the lobby floor.

Destiny and the bigfoot took the stairs two at a time. She opened the lobby door and saw her neighbor run out into the street, shouting something, her hands raised over her head.

They followed after her. A crowd was starting to gather as Mr. Mather, who lived in the building across the street, pulled her into his arms.

Destiny and her beast stopped on the top steps. Now it seemed like everyone was looking at them.

"He's got Sweet D!" Mrs. Hobbes cried before fainting dead away.

Now Destiny was really confused. What did she mean by that? Who got her?

Her beast stepped back and she lost her grip on its hand.

Benny Ortiz who Destiny's mom said was head of a gang but he always was nice to Destiny, pointed at her beast and shouted, "Who the fuck are you, man? You touch D?"

"Leave him alone," Destiny said. "He's my beast and no one else can have him."

Benny's friends seemed to pop out of the shadows and surrounded Destiny and her beast. They all looked very, very angry.

"You picked the wrong girl to mess with, bro," Benny said, cracking his knuckles. The streetlight caught the two tattooed teardrops under his eye. Destiny didn't like the way he was talking to her beast.

"We were just playing," Destiny whined, but even she realized no one was going to listen to her.

Her beast tried to walk away but was blocked by three of Benny's friends. When it turned around, four more got in the way. Destiny felt a rough hand take her by the wrist and drag her away. It was Benny.

"No! Leave him alone. He's my friend."

Benny said, "I need you to turn away, Sweet D. Can you do that for me?" He was talking all soft and nice, but she saw the bad in his eyes.

Destiny did as she was told, fighting back tears. It seemed like the entire neighborhood was out watching her. A few people shouted, "Kick his ass!"

Why was everyone being so mean to her beast?

When she tried to turn around to tell her beast to run, Benny got ahold of her shoulders and kept her pointed to the building across the street.

"Do him," Benny said to his friends.

And that's when the sounds of punching and kicking started.

CHAPTER TWENTY-ONE

Being the alpha predator all its life, the bigfoot had no idea what to do in a situation when it was attacked by many of the large things that were not the least bit afraid of it. The gang, twelve angry young men in all, jumped the sasquatch as one furious mass. They kicked at its knees and crotch, punched it in the kidneys, stomach, face and neck.

When a boot connected with the open wound in its leg, the bigfoot let loose with a piteous roar that caused the gang to stop.

"What the fuck?" one of the guys said, his arm cocked back and ready to deliver another blow to the sasquatch's head.

"Must be a recording or something in the suit," Benny said. "Take his fucking mask off!"

The gang regained their momentum, this time focusing on the bigfoot's head and neck. Grabbing tufts of hair, they pulled and yanked and twisted. The bigfoot fell to its knees.

"It's not coming off!"

"Keep trying," Benny barked.

Destiny wailed. "Please stop! Leave my beast alone!"

She broke free from Benny and caught the bigfoot's eye. For a moment, between the pulling and punching, the bigfoot reached out for her. She tried to run to its aid, but Benny snagged her by the waist.

"Motherfucker smells like the dump," one of the gang members griped as he kicked it in the base of its spine, pitching the great beast forward.

"I think he shit himself," another joked.

They continued to rain blows on Destiny's beast. Her mother, hearing the commotion, had rushed outside and took her from Benny.

"They're hurting my friend," Destiny said to her mother, her eyes shimmering with tears.

"I...I..."

"This freak was touching Destiny," Benny said.

"He was not!" Destiny shot back.

People in the crowd were yelling to call the police, while others were urging on the beating as if it were a pay per view boxing match. Over a hundred people had swarmed from their apartments to watch. Even little kids dressed as fairies and pirates stared on, wondering what all the fuss was about.

And beneath it all, the bigfoot absorbed their rage and felt the world around it go from gray to black.

Shay was in the middle of texting a reply to Katie when he heard the roar of a crowd the next block over. "That sounds really bad."

Vito shoved his phone in his back pocket. "No shit. I hope it's about our bigfoot and not something else that might get us killed for sticking our noses in."

"Well, there's only one way to find out." Shay jogged up the block. No matter what he did from here on, he felt like a man trudging down death row. Death by sasquatch might be preferable to what he'd have to face when he got home.

They turned the corner and beheld what would look like a giant block party if not for the raucous shouts of 'beat his ass!' Pushing their way through the mob, they stumbled into the cleared perimeter where a whole lot of guys were laying a beat down on someone Shay couldn't make out in the dark and cluster of bodies.

When one of them stepped back to bend over and puke, the smell came hurtling towards Shay's nose. He didn't need to see their victim to know what they were roughing up.

"Christ, they got him," Shay said.

A tall girl with long, braided hair was sobbing, trying to run toward the bigfoot, but she was held back by a woman who may or may not have been her mother and another guy. "You're killing him! He never did anything to you! Stop hurting him!"

Shay looked to Vito. "What do you think that's all about?"

Vito stared at the spectacle, his mouth catching flies. "I have no freaking clue."

The huge beast lay on its back as the men kicked it over and over. It wasn't even flinching with each blow.

They killed it, Shay thought. In a way, that should be a relief. The Bronx always took care of its own. He and Vito could go home, take their licks, and try to put this all behind them. No more bigfoot, no more carnage. Maybe they could make an anonymous donation to some of the families that had lost loved ones today. Well, when Shay had any spare money to give.

But it wasn't that easy. Nothing in Shay's life ever was.

He was responsible for this great and mysterious creature lying dead on a dirty sidewalk. For the lives lost and property damage. For the crying girl who looked desperate to be beside the bigfoot. The more Shay watched and listened to her, the more he realized she had to be mentally impaired, and suddenly, her crying riding over the cacophony of the mob, his heart broke.

Maybe, just maybe, it wasn't dead.

And if that was the case...

"We have to get it out of here."

"I don't think they make body bags that big," Vito said. Shay was about to tell him he wasn't messing around when his friend added, "I know what you mean. But how the hell do we stop them?"

Shay and Vito were no shrinking violets, but they knew they were no match against a gang. The creeps pounding on the bigfoot were most certainly a gang, judging by their matching clothes – tight black jeans and black North Face jackets – and pretty damn similar haircuts. Shay would lay down money that if he could see their arms or necks, they would each sport identical tattoos.

"We could pretend we're cops," Shay said.

It wouldn't be a stretch. In the game of 'what doesn't belong', they stood out like sore thumbs. It would be easy to announce they were plainclothes cops who just happened to have left their badges and guns at home.

Vito shot that idea down quickly. "No way. They'll trade bigfoot for us if we do that."

A thought flickered in Shay's mind that would die of loneliness if he didn't run with it. "Well, we could try the truth for once."

"Are you nuts?"

"It's so crazy, it might just get them to stop. Follow my lead."

Shay's stomach had turned to water. Every instinct was telling him to get his lily-white ass out of there.

In a loud voice, he shouted over the crowd, "All right, that's enough! Animal control! Please, I need you to back away from the animal."

A pair of gangsters stopped what they were doing and whipped around toward Shay. "The fuck you say?" one of them said. His eyes were glassy either from drugs or the endorphin rush from laying down a beating.

Shay hoped no one could hear him swallow hard enough to hurt. "That animal you're, ah, kicking, was reported missing by…by the Big Apple Circus." Was the circus even still a thing? Shay hadn't a clue, but he was committed to it. "I, I need everyone to step back."

"That's not an animal, puta," the guy holding onto the crying girl said. "Why don't you get your ass out of here. You don't know shit."

His rectum puckering, Shay drew a breath and replied, "Sure looks like an animal to me. In fact, the very same animal we were sent to bring back."

"It's an asshole in a suit," the guy spat back. "You need to turn your ass around and get to steppin'."

Shay noticed a few gang members tugging on the bigfoot's head, ostensibly attempting to remove its so-called mask. "Not having any luck with that?"

"We can assure you, it's not a man in a costume," Vito added. "More importantly, it can be very dangerous."

"Don't look too dangerous now, does it?" the guy said.

No, it didn't. It looked quite dead. Shay dared to step closer. "It's a very rare animal that you might have heard of."

This was it. Shay was going to see if a little shock and awe worked.

"Well, what is it?" someone from the crowd asked.

He looked at Vito and then back across the sea of angry faces, with the exception of the pretty crying girl. "That's a bigfoot. And we need to get it back to where it belongs."

What followed was a burst of laughter that would have tripled Shay's ego if he had been trying his hand at stand up comedy.

"Bigfoot! You crazy!"

"Hey, someone get some beef jerky!"

"These motherfuckers must be smoking crack!"

"Get the hell outta here, stupid!"

"Sasquatch gonna get ya!"

Shay felt himself redden. On the flip side, they had stopped wailing on the sasquatch. He cringed when he looked at the creature. Its face was a swollen, bloody mess. He could only imagine the kind of internal injuries it had suffered. Its fur was smeared with what looked like blue paste. That made zero sense to him, but he was in the no-sense zone now.

I'm such an asshole, he thought. *All this over money. What the hell was I thinking?*

Close enough to kneel next to the fallen cryptid, he dared himself to reach out and touch its shoulder. He studied its chest to see if it was breathing. He didn't realize Vito was standing over him until he heard him say, "Oh man, it's dead."

That gave Shay another idea. He pressed his fingers against what little bit of a neck the Bigfoot possessed.

"He's dead," he said loud enough for those around him to hear. "Vito, I need you to call it in."

Vito didn't move for a moment, his eyes searching for any clue as to what Shay intended.

"Let them know we need the morgue to get here, STAT!" Shay belched. He wanted to give Vito a wink but he didn't dare let anyone in on the ploy. Did anyone say they needed a morgue STAT? It sounded like TV bullshit, but so what.

Finally, Vito said, "Right." He checked his phone before dialing and said, "I guess estimated time of death is seven-thirty-five."

Now the murmurs started.

"He's dead."

"Shit, he died."

"I'm outta here."

As soon as Vito put the phone to his ear and started talking about needing a body pickup, people scattered like cockroaches when the lights turn on. The gang members took flight instantly. In less than a minute, Shay and Vito were pretty much alone with the bigfoot corpse, except for the crying girl, her mother and the gang banger who had been helping hold her back. She collapsed next to the bigfoot and stroked its wounded forehead.

"He never did anything to anyone," she wept. "He was my beast and they took him away!"

"Come on inside, Destiny," her mother said, trying to lift her up by her arms. "This is no place for us. We'll talk about it inside."

"No! I'm not leaving him."

"I'll carry her inside if you need me to," the gang guy said. This guy was hard to read. On one hand, he had his boys beat the bigfoot to death. On the other, he seemed to really care about the girl's welfare. That was a puzzle to sort out for another day, if ever.

Shay had no idea how this girl had formed a special bond with the bigfoot in so short a time. Again, it was further proof that the creature was more than just a wild animal.

A wild animal that would never again roam the woods.

Vito leaned into Shay and whispered, "Who should I really call now?"

"I guess the police."

Shay was just like the gang members. He didn't want to be anywhere near here when the cops arrived. He would leave feeling better that the bigfoot wouldn't hurt anyone else, yet burdened by guilt. It seemed a small price to pay for his greed and stupidity.

Unless…

He'd been wrong about the bigfoot being dead before.

Checking it for any kind of vitals again, he shrugged the thought away.

The girl fought against her mother and the gang banger as they attempted to pry her away from the sasquatch. "Leave me alone! I hate you!"

Vito tapped Shay on the shoulder and they stepped back. There was nothing else they could do.

"Please come back!" the girl howled. "Please!"

Pushing her mother away with a stiff arm – boy, the girl was strong – she pounded on the bigfoot's chest with the other.

"Come on, we should go," Vito said.

"Yeah."

The girl brought her fist down in the center of the sasquatch's chest.

The huge beast let out a terrific gasp. Its eyes flew open, rolling for a bit until they found the crying girl. A smile warmed her face and she yelled, "He's back! My beast is back!"

Then the bigfoot turned its head and locked on the gang banger.

It was on its feet in seconds. Shay jumped back as if he were leaping over a downed, live wire.

"You wanna go?" the gang banger said as he pulled out a pistol.

He didn't have time to slip his finger on the trigger. In a flash, the bigfoot stormed the space between them and punched the guy in the stomach.

What made Shay lose his lunch, breakfast and a hundred dinners was the way the sasquatch's fist went all the way through the guy's body, punching out the back, sending forth a bloody shower of bone, shredded organs and other unpleasant meat.

The bigfoot waved its arm up and down, shaking more viscera from the hole in his back.

And to everyone's horror, the gang banger was still alive.

"F..f...fuck...yo...you," he sputtered. Blood bubbled out of his mouth in a horrid froth.

"Oh Lord, Benny," the girl's mother cried. She grabbed the girl's hand and ran into the apartment building. The girl resisted at first, until a thick blob of blood hit her in the face.

It appeared the bigfoot was getting frustrated at being stuck inside the man. It grabbed him by the face, its meaty hand covering his entire head, and pulled it from his neck as freely as if it were plucking a daisy.

Dozens of people watching from their windows screamed. There were cries of, "It killed Benny! It killed Benny!"

With his head gone and now rolling until it bounced off a car tire, the body went limp and slipped right off the bigfoot's wet arm.

Why aren't we running? Shay thought as the snarling beast turned to them. *We should be running. Godammit, why are we just standing here?*

Part of it was shock at witnessing a display of unthinkable violence. Part of it was disbelief that the bigfoot was still alive, though it shouldn't have surprised him.

Fool me once, shame on you. Fool me twice, well, fuck, this is just insane.

But the most important part was that Shay had now been close enough to see what Vito saw when he looked in its eyes.

By all means, the bigfoot should want to turn them into so much chop meat. In fact, Shay and Vito should be skewered on each arm by now.

The bigfoot looked to them not with malice, but with an almost pleading cry to help it. It wobbled on its feet for a moment, and then collapsed in the middle of the street.

The cops would surely be coming soon now.

"We have to get it out of here," Shay said.

"Did you not see what it just did to that dude?"

"I sure did. I'll never be able to un-see it. But now I know what you meant earlier."

"We can't carry it and I'm fresh out of pocket wheelbarrows."

The bigfoot moved its legs. It looked like it was trying to get up.

"Maybe we can help get it on its feet and get the heck out of here."

Vito's jaw pulsed. "Every time you make a plan, things get worse."

"Which means I'm overdue for a bit of good fortune. You get one side."

They each grabbed an arm and tugged until the cords in their necks were as taut as the supports on the George Washington Bridge. The bigfoot stirred and was able to give just enough help to get itself vertical. Vito and Shay draped an arm over their shoulders. Shay felt the intense weight and power of the beast and realized it could crush him with ease. He tried desperately to push that thought away.

"Well, Sherlock, where to now?" Vito asked, huffing from the exertion.

"That way. We need to get this guy somewhere we can stash him and come back with your truck."

"I'm not putting it in my truck again!"

They walked with the beast between them, the bigfoot dragging its feet but at least it was walking and not murdering them.

"We have to take him back to where he lives."

"You're out of your fucking mind."

Shay realized he'd gotten used to the bigfoot's musk. That could be a sign his olfactory sense had committed suicide.

He didn't have the strength to argue with Vito. They walked down the street and made a left, leaving the bloody scene behind them.

As they turned the corner, they spotted a huge cluster of trick or treaters.

And they were headed right for them.

CHAPTER TWENTY-TWO

As soon as Vito saw all of the kids in their costumes, his heart sank. It would be impossible to pass the beaten and bloody bigfoot off as just a very tall man in a strange costume. The mouse over the creature's left eye had swollen to the point of splitting open. Stuff Vito preferred not to think of or dwell upon pushed out of the seam like pink oatmeal.

Vito looked behind them and saw more kids coming the other way. Why did it have to be Halloween?

Because you're being punished, stupid. This is what you get for stealing.

No matter what, maneuvering the wounded, lumbering giant in anything other than a straight line was no easy task. Vito's shoulders and legs were already feeling the burn. Shay's must have been on fire.

"Maybe we should set it down somewhere in the dark and I'll run and get my truck."

Puffing as he spoke, Shay said, "Looks like traffic on Jerome is still a parking lot. You won't get through."

"Yeah, well, we're not getting through those kids, either. And I'm about to collapse."

"I guess it can't hurt to take a break."

Shay and Vito tried to settle the bigfoot in a corner by some stairs leading up to a two-family home, but once they relaxed, gravity grabbed onto the creature and unceremoniously yanked it to the ground. Vito heard its skull thwack off the concrete wall and his own head felt a sharp sympathy pain.

They skittered back, both afraid the sudden fall would fully awaken the cryptid and send it into a rage. Its one good eye rolled a bit, but it stayed down and partially out.

"It's gonna…have some knot…on its head," Shay said, as winded as a marathoner.

"That's the least of its freaking worries. And ours. Man, there's no way we're going to get it back to my truck."

"Maybe we just wait a bit until traffic gets moving again. Then you can get your truck."

"Did you see the destruction back there? And there's a multiple car wreck and murder scene. It'll be three in the morning before the police open things up."

By three a.m., they would both be on the way to divorce and the bigfoot would most likely regain some strength and be back on the prowl. Vito made a promise to God that if they got out of this with their lives and wives, he would never hunt or harm another animal again. Not that he harmed many when he hunted, but it was the principle that counted.

The first group of kids walked by. They were tweens or early teens, more interested in their phones than the slumbering giant. Vito and Shay stood in front of the bigfoot, hiding it as best they could.

Smaller kids walking with their parents came by. A little boy dressed as a cowboy said to them, "Trick or treat." He stopped and held his plastic pumpkin out to them.

"Sorry, I don't have any candy," Shay said. "But I hear that building has a ton of candy." He pointed to the apartment building down the street.

You'd think he'd told the kid his dog had died. He looked up at Vito and Shay with tears in his eyes.

"Come on, Jose, not everyone celebrates Halloween," a woman dressed as a prison guard in a soft-core porn flick said.

"No candy?" the boy said.

"Time to go," the woman said. "Don't bother with those grinches."

Grinches? Since when did asking people on the street for treats fall within the rules of Halloween? And the Grinch was a Christmas thing.

Vito whipped out his wallet, plucked a dollar out and tucked it into the boy's pumpkin. "Here you go. Happy Halloween, buckaroo."

It was a minor miscalculation on his part. Now all of the kids circled him like seagulls on a dock, asking for a dollar. He certainly didn't have enough to go around. They pressed closer until a girl in a princess get up said, "What's that?"

She pointed at the bigfoot with one hand over her mouth.

"Just a sleepy gorilla," Shay said unevenly.

One of the fathers came closer and said, "Oh shit, that looks like the dude who fucked up those stores."

Vito wanted to remind the guy he was around a bunch of kids and should probably watch his mouth. Even shitting bricks, he couldn't quell his paternal instincts.

"I think he's right," a woman not wearing a costume chimed in.

"Somebody call the cops."

"This isn't the guy," Shay said. "I saw him. He went down Gun Hill Road, headed to Webster."

This crowd wasn't buying it. Vito was doling out bills, but the kids weren't moving along.

"Somebody fucked him up," the father of the year said.

"But why is the costume looking all jacked?" another guy asked.

That's the question that's going to get us in a whole lot of trouble, Vito thought. *Please, take your kids and go!*

The trashy prison guard shoved past Vito and got a closer look. "Guys, I don't think that's a costume."

"You been hitting that wax pen?"

"No, look, I'm serious."

Now the rest of the adults and kids walked through Vito and Shay as if they didn't exist. What the heck could they say to end their curiosity?

"Smells like he messed himself," a boy said.

A chorus of 'eewwwww' rose from the group.

The bigfoot stirred. It put its palms flat on the ground and pushed itself from the wall it was leaning against.

The eeewwwws turned to dog whistle screeches.

"I told you it's not a costume! Look!"

Blood pooled out of the bigfoot's mouth and it sneezed on the crowd, showering them with mucous and blood. Now even the adults were yelping, everyone backing away.

"Police! Police!" a woman shouted loud enough to be heard in Queens.

"Don't do that," Vito said in vain. He saw a cop two blocks up turn their way.

All of the screaming was like smelling salts for the bigfoot. It got to its feet, towering over everyone.

"Do we run for it?" Shay said, hopping from foot to foot.

The parents finally hustled their kids away. The commotion had the other waves of trick or treaters heading across the street like an impromptu parade.

Settling its eye on Shay and Vito, the bigfoot grunted. Vito had no way of knowing what that grunt meant. Its lone eye was tearing blood and did not look happy to see them.

The cop was almost on them. When he saw the bigfoot, he drew his gun and said to them, "I need you to step back."

"Wait, officer, you don't understand," Vito said.

"That wasn't a request. Get back, now!"

His pistol was pointed at the bigfoot. He keyed the walkie clipped to his shoulder. "I have our suspect. Request backup immediately."

The bigfoot glowered at the cop.

"Officer, I think you're just making it madder," Shay said. "It doesn't want to harm anyone."

"It's hurt and it's scared," Vito said.

The cop, a young guy who looked like he was trying to grow his first mustache, looked at them as if they'd fallen out of a coconut tree sprouting from the dirty sidewalk. "It looks *real* scared. Now back off and shut up."

Clenching its fists, the bigfoot bellowed so loud, Vito felt his organs shift.

The cop's eyes went as big and white as ping pong balls and he pulled the trigger.

Vito saw a tuft of hair on the bigfoot's shoulder puff into the air, followed by a spattering of blood.

The bigfoot closed the gap between it and the officer in two strides and backhanded the man before he could get off another shot. He hit into a parked car hard enough to dent the door and shatter the window.

Vito grabbed Shay's arm, ready to beat feet if the creature was going to turn on them next. He spied more cops running down the street.

"Calm down, buddy. It's going to be okay," he said to the bigfoot in as soft and even a tone as he could muster. It was awful hard to do when your teeth were chattering.

It gave them a quick glimpse, but then turned its attention to the rapidly approaching police.

It should have wacked Vito and Shay. They deserved it.

Instead, it bolted, making a bee-line for the cops.

"Don't shoot! Don't shoot!" Vito said, waving his arms. Shay did the same.

The bigfoot barreled into them as if they were bowling pins, scattering them like breadcrumbs.

"Let's go," Vito said, taking off after the bigfoot.

"What about him?" Shay said, pointing to the unconscious cop.

"I can guarantee an ambulance will be here soon. There's nothing we can do for him. Come on!"

Even if they had lost sight of the bigfoot, they could follow its every move by the screams. Pedestrians were batted aside. Hopefully none of them were hurt too bad.

When the bigfoot got to Jerome Avenue, it looked to its left and darted right. Vito saw more police in pursuit.

The creature took to the middle of the road. It jumped onto the hood of a car snarled in traffic and proceeded to crunch all the cars behind it like stepping stones.

With so many people around, Vito was relieved that the cops couldn't start shooting like it was a wild western show. Ten officers tried their best to keep up. Vito and Shay were just slightly ahead of them, running alongside the trail of stopped cars and trucks.

Metal crushed and glass exploded as the bigfoot gained more ground. People in their cars saw what was coming and doors flew open, vomiting their passengers.

As Vito got more and more winded, he started to wonder why he and Shay were still trying to save the bigfoot. They couldn't keep up with it for much longer. It was causing a pile of carnage. And he and Shay were not bulletproof. If the cops wanted to take it down in a hail of gunfire, they were going to be of little use.

Because this is our fault. We have to keep going until we can't anymore. Would Danielle be proud of him, or call him a world class idiot for letting Shay talk him into lugging the bigfoot home?

The latter, for sure.

Horns honked while people on the sidewalks stopped to watch the spectacle. Quite a few phones were out recording everything.

Bigfoot was about to be very real to the entire world.

Just as a needling stitch started jabbing his side, Vito's eyes went wide when the bigfoot stopped pouncing on cars and headed for the stairs leading up to the subway platform.

"Jesus, Mary and Joseph, not the subway," Shay opined behind him.

They hit the stairs and heard the rumble of feet as people on the platform panicked.

"One thing's…for sure," Shay blurted.

"What's that?" Vito thought his heart was going to gallop through his chest.

"It won't get far…without a…MetroCard."

CHAPTER TWENTY-THREE

Shay's attempt at humor fell flatter than his wallet. That was fine by him. He needed a release valve. Stress always boosted his wise-cracking quotient, and right now, his stress level was off the rails. He hoped the bigfoot didn't do the same to one of the trains.

They clambered up the steps and were immediately shoved back by a sea of people fleeing the hairy wrecking ball. Shay just managed to get a hold on the handrail, barely preventing him from flipping backwards down the metal stairs. He saw the police at the bottom trying to swim upstream to no avail.

"Don't hurt my beast!" a shrill voice shouted above the din.

It was that girl from the gang beating. She must have gotten away from her mother – which was no surprise, considering she was twice the size of the woman. He thought he'd heard her mother call her Destiny. He hoped being savaged by a sasquatch *was not* her destiny. Even though there appeared to be something special between them, the creature was in a place loaded with things it didn't understand, and when it was spooked, well, the results were never good.

Where the police were attempting to politely navigate around the panicked public, the girl plowed through them with enviable single-minded purpose.

"Just great."

"What?" Vito said, clinging to the rail opposite him. Shay pointed at Destiny. Vito gave him a look that said, *why not? Everything else has gone wrong to this point.*

As the crowd thinned to a trickle at the top of the platform, Shay and Vito were able to muscle through. The bigfoot stood at the far end, looking down at the tracks.

"Maybe we should approach it slowly. Don't want to spook it any more than it already is," Shay said.

Vito checked their back and the police making their way slowly but surely up the steps. "I don't think they're going to make it so easy."

The girl made it to the top and hip-checked Shay hard enough to send him into the rail.

"Beast! It's me! Destiny!"

Vito managed to grab onto her wrist to keep her from rushing headlong to her death. She fought against him, but he held tight.

Ribs sore, Shay said, "Destiny, I need you to calm down. We're on the same team…I think."

She spun around and clobbered Vito on the side of his head with an open hand slap that echoed down the tracks. Instantly free, she sprinted to the sasquatch.

Vito rubbed the side of his reddening face. There was a tear in his eye. "Holy crap. It's like getting hit with a two-by-four."

"We'll put a raw steak on it later. We have to stop her."

They raced after Destiny, though her age and fresh legs gave her a distinct advantage.

Shay felt rumbling beneath his feet and turned to see the police had finally made the party. He counted seven in all.

"Running from the cops on Halloween was a lot more fun when we were kids," Shay said.

Vito's faced screwed up tight and he found another gear, pulling away from Shay.

"No problem. I've got…got your back."

Destiny was only five feet from the battered bigfoot when Vito nearly tackled her at the waist. Shay instantly realized that had not been a good idea. The bigfoot, which had watched Destiny's approach with a blank stare, grew enraged when it saw Vito knock her down.

"Vito, get the hell back!" Shay screamed in a falsetto he didn't know he possessed.

The sasquatch swiped at the empty air where Vito had been before rolling off the girl. Now on his ass, he scuttled backwards, trying to keep a safe distance from those meaty hands. Shay reached him and dragged him back even further.

The bigfoot puffed up its chest and roared in their direction, its displeasure painted all over its puffy, bloodied face.

Destiny had rocketed back onto her feet and wedged herself between man and sasquatch.

"You shouldn't yell," she admonished it.

To Shay's amazement, the bigfoot took notice of her and deflated instantly. It regarded her with a single, sad eye.

"Police!"

Shay spun around. Seven guns for seven cops were pointed at the bigfoot.

And the girl.

"You can't shoot," Shay said to them. "You'll kill her."

Vito stood and put his hands up, slowly walking toward the police. "Everyone needs to chill out."

"Miss, I need you to slowly walk to me," one of the cops said.

"No! I'm not going to let you take my beast away!"

When she reached for the creature's hand, Shay's heart skipped more beats than it hit. "Don't do that!" he said.

The bigfoot let her. It craned its neck and came close to touching her forehead with its own.

"See, it's calm now," Vito said. "Call animal control or something. Maybe you can tranquilize it."

Shay rubbed his eyes. He remembered a line from the original King Kong.

It was beauty that killed the beast.

The girl was definitely a beauty. He just hoped the bigfoot had a better fate than Kong. Destiny. Fate. It would have made Shay chuckle in any other circumstance.

The cops kept demanding they all step away from the creature and Vito tried to talk them down. The problem was, they had seen what the bigfoot had done in just a couple of hours and they were trained not to take any chances.

Destiny spoke soothingly to the bigfoot, telling it how she was going to take it home and it could eat her other Rainbow Dash if it wanted to. The beast kept flicking wary glances at the police, but it seemed happy to stay still and not destroy anything as long as Destiny was near.

He heard one of the cops get on his radio and ask for animal control to get there right away and to treat it as if they had a bear cornered on the subway platform. Another cop said, "I say we take care of it here and now."

Vito said, "You can't…"

The squeal and rattle of an approaching train drowned out the rest of what he was going to say.

The metallic caterwauling of the train spooked the bigfoot. The creature pulled away from Destiny.

Seconds later, the train came to a stop. The previous mayor had done a great job cleaning up the subways, but this car was like a relic from the past. Every square inch of the exterior was covered in illegible graffiti.

The doors opened and the people who had been standing by them to get out rushed back inside when they saw the bigfoot. Muffled screams from inside the train car became clear as an air raid siren as everyone ran out of the other door further up the car. Again, the police were swamped by the crush of humanity.

Shay watched the bigfoot dip into the train, Destiny close behind.

He and Vito jumped in the other door to the car. The only person between them and the bigfoot was a homeless man too drunk to fathom what was going on around him. He looked to the sasquatch, and then dipped his head until his chin touched his chest and he was out.

Shay jumped when the door closed behind them and the train started moving.

"This is bad," he said. "So, so, so bad."

They were trapped in a mobile tin can with an angry creature of the wild.

"Not if she can keep it quiet," Vito said.

Destiny said something about her mother being mad if she found out she took a train ride without her. But then she saw the confusion on the bigfoot's face and told it everything would be all right and riding trains was fun.

Riding a New York subway was never fun, Shay thought. Especially not with a bigfoot on board.

The train rattled and shook. Shay had to hang on to one of the overhead bars to remain on his feet.

"Well, now what do we do?" Shay asked Vito.

"Riding the 4 train wasn't exactly something I'd considered."

No matter what Destiny said to the bigfoot, the movement of the train was keeping the sasquatch on edge. It peered at Shay and Vito and for a flash looked like it wanted to turn them into an appetizer.

"I don't like her being so close," Shay said. "Sure, it's calm when she's around, but it doesn't look like it'll take much to put it in total freak out mode. If it does, she's in a whole mess of trouble."

The homeless man blubbered, "Serves you right, you sumbitch!" while he slept.

The door behind them slammed open and, of course, the cops were there.

"What is it with this chick and that thing?" an older cop with a cleft chin deep enough to store his keys within said. Then he swiveled to Shay and Vito and added, "And why are you two mixed up in this?"

Shay was about to sputter the best lie he could come up with when the train took a sharp turn. An officer's gun went off into the floor of the train by accident.

The bigfoot trumpeted a warning sign to clear the hell out. Shay would swear the train's windows shook.

Destiny said, "You better not shoot my beast! If you hurt him, I'll be very, very mad."

And she looked it, too.

The bigfoot had other plans. It jumped up onto a pair of seats, cracking the thick plastic. It started pounding on the ceiling. The sound hurt Shay's ears. Even Destiny was alarmed because she backed away, covering her ears. Vito dodged around Shay and scooped her up in his arms. This time she didn't fight.

"Stop it! Too loud!" she yelled at the bigfoot, or as she kept referring to it, her beast.

Shay saw that the cops were ready to take aim and fire, even with Vito and Destiny partially in the way.

This might be the dumbest thing I'm ever going to do.

He started jumping up and down and waving his arms. It had been ages since he'd done a jumping jack. It was supposed to be good for your health, though in this instance, it could be the exact opposite.

"Get down, you fucking idiot," one of the cops barked.

"Everyone shut up!" the homeless drunk said, his eyes still closed.

The bigfoot pounded and pounded until metal screeched and tore. Shay whipped around and couldn't believe it. The creature had actually punched a hole through the roof of the subway car.

It took one last, longing look at Destiny and then pulled itself up through the hole and onto the roof.

Destiny reached out for it, wailing, "Nooooooo!"

The police started shooting into the ceiling. The sound was deafening. Shay dropped to the grimy floor and covered his head while the train swayed back and forth, heading straight for hell.

CHAPTER TWENTY-FOUR

Vito held onto Destiny as best he could. It was like trying to wrestle a marlin onboard a rolling ship. She jabbed him with flying elbows and wild kicks. She wanted to go up after the bigfoot but he could not let that happen. This poor, deluded girl, actually, a woman, may have some strange bond with the bigfoot, but right now, she needed more looking after than the creature.

"A little help, Shay!" he shouted over the gunfire.

Shay looked up with terror-filled eyes.

Vito was on the floor, wrestling against Destiny. If she didn't kill herself falling off the roof of the train, she would definitely take a bullet.

"Dude!" Vito snapped.

Shay crawled to them on his stomach.

"Grab her legs," Vito said.

Taking a knee to the chin for his efforts, Shay wrapped his arms around her calves and rode them like a cowboy on a bronco.

The roof of the subway car sprouted great indentations as the bigfoot ran across it, gunfire following its movement. Vito's ears were ringing and every muscle hurt as he attempted to corral the girl.

The pounding footsteps stopped and Vito realized it had moved on to the next car. He thought he could hear the few people trapped in it scream. The police yanked the door back and clambered into the other car.

The fight instantly left Destiny without warning. One second she was like an angry tiger, and the next she was softly sobbing, her limbs gone limp.

"I want my mom. I wanna go home," she said between hitching whimpers.

Vito rocked her in his arms. "It's okay. Shhhh, shhhh. We'll get you home. Don't worry."

Shay released her legs and rolled onto his back, panting and rubbing his chin while he gawked at the foot indentations in the ceiling. "I hurt way too much for this to just be a nightmare."

The distant sounds of shots being fired made Vito and Shay flinch.

"Change of plans," Vito said. "We have to get this girl home."

Shaw tested his jaw. "I hear you."

Destiny's cries lessened until she was just about asleep. Vito's heart broke for the girl. Her mother must be worried half to death. He couldn't imagine how he would feel if Meredith had run away from them to be with a monster.

The three of them lay exhausted on the floor while the homeless man snored.

The bigfoot would have stopped running if not for the bee stings to the bottom of its feet and legs. It was dizzy and hurt and tired and just wanted to go back to the small/big thing.

The 4 train lumbered on. The sky was crisp and clear, but with so many less lights than back home.

Home.

Even though it wanted to stop, it had to keep moving to find home.

Its face hurt from the biting wind. Whatever fog had settled on its brain was gone, but now its vision was hampered by only having one eye not swollen enough to see out of.

The wounds in its leg and shoulder throbbed with each beat of its frantic heart. Add to that the new agonies, especially on its feet. The pain kept it going while also threatening to pull it under.

More bees came flying from the ground.

It needed to get away from the bees.

It needed to find home.

The train came to a lurching stop.

The bigfoot lost its footing. It tumbled across the roof, slipping over the end and wedging itself between two cars.

Desperate to get away, it quickly extracted itself, jumped off the stopped train and found itself confronted with many, many more big things. Like all of the others in this place, they raised their voices and ran. It bellowed after them, hurrying them away.

It hated the big things in this place that was not home.

All except one.

The stairs were clogged with bodies, so the bigfoot leaped onto an L pillar, shimmying down until it was on the street. Cars swerved to avoid it, slamming into other cars and unwary pedestrians.

There were so many more lights and big things here. The brightness hurt its eye and compelled it to keep going.

Limping because one of its feet had taken on too many bee stings, it jogged down the path, bumping into large things, swinging wildly to get them out of its way.

A strange yet familiar scent was in the air.

The bigfoot latched onto the faint aroma.

Home?

It couldn't be sure.

But it had something to follow now. A purpose. An end to this horrible day.

Vito had managed to get Destiny into a seat with Shay's help. She was complete dead weight, sleeping as soundly as the drunk. He looked out the grimy window and sighed. "It's running down Fordham Road."

"Of course it is."

Shay rested his knees on a seat and pressed his face against the window.

Fordham Road was the shopping capital of the Bronx. Stores of every shape and size lined the sidewalks, hawking high-end sneakers, electronics, discount clothes and stationery stores galore. Vito's mother used to take him to Fordham Road to get his shoes for school way back when he went to a Catholic High School with Shay. If there was a bargain to be had, you'd find it on Fordham Road.

The creature couldn't have found a more populated place to run rampant.

He watched the bigfoot stagger/run, parting the crowd like Moses and the Red Sea. Even those who thought he was a man in costume must have been alarmed by his sheer size and physical condition.

"Is she hurt?"

Vito snapped his head around to find a cop cautiously entering the subway car.

"No. She's asleep. I think this was all too much for her."

"You sure?" the cop kept eyeing the hole in the ceiling.

"It's out there if that's what you're worried about," Shay said, tapping the window.

"Can you help us get her home?" Vito said.

"We might need her for questioning."

Vito bristled. "Then you'll have to get her home and talk to her mother or guardian. You won't be able to do a thing with her without her permission."

The cop apparently had no idea what Vito was implying, but he helped them anyway without further word. Vito roused Destiny and she walked between him and Shay onto the platform and then down the stairs. It was bedlam down below, but she was too tired to care anymore.

They were met by a pair of officers. Vito told them where he was sure the girl lived and how she came to be on the train with the bigfoot as he best could put things together. He could tell the police were more interested in how he and Shay fit into everything.

"Wrong place at the wrong time," Shay said under the flaring police lights. "We just wanted to make sure the girl was safe."

Vito appreciated his friend's ability to be fast on his feet and saving their bacon. The police had far more pressing matters, anyway.

They walked Destiny to a cop car. She was groggy but alert enough to ask, "Am I in trouble?"

"No, sweetie. These nice policemen are going to take you home to your mom. Okay?" Vito said.

She nodded, her lids heavy.

"Please tell my beast I said hi and to come over tomorrow to play."

The door was closed before Vito could answer her. Destiny leaned her head against the window and the car slowly drove through the crowd.

Vito looked at his phone. The texts from Danielle were not happy or nice. Shay did the same with his phone and winced.

A neon sign for a bar called The Joint called to them. "I need a drink," Vito said.

"Yeah, me too. Or ten."

The Joint was nestled between a cell phone store and a Jamaican fast food restaurant. When the bar door closed behind them, Vito exhaled for the first time in hours. It was a blessing to be away from the chaos and lights and crowds. He ordered two double whiskies, neat.

The place was empty save one patron. Vito assumed everyone had left to see firsthand what had happened.

"Some crazy shit going down out there," an elderly man who looked like he was attached to his barstool said as he watched the television above the bar.

It was tuned to the news filled with live action reporting of the strange animal that had terrorized the Bronx. A helicopter followed the bigfoot's mad dash. Seeing it trapped in the harsh glare of the spotlight, running down cracked sidewalks that must have seemed so alien to it, Vito downed the drink in one gulp. "Craziest shit anyone here will ever see."

Shay's drink was gone just as fast and Vito ordered another round.

They sat in silence because really, what could they possibly say? Their minds, just as much as their bodies, were fried.

On the television, an off camera anchor described the damages and deaths attributed to the wild creature. On the screen, red and white flashing lights attempted to cut the bigfoot off. It was too smart for them, hopping what looked to be a ten-foot fence and running diagonally down the block, avoiding the barricade.

A part of Vito cheered the bigfoot on.

"Boy, did we fuck up," Shay said into his glass.

"That's putting it mildly."

They sipped their whiskies and watched the news. Vito felt the booze burn a hole in his gut.

He was about to order another round when Shay slapped his palm on the bar. "I know where it's going!"

"That's amazing, but I don't think *it* even does."

"I'll lay anything down that it's headed for the one place that will seem most like where it lives."

The edges of Vito's brain had gotten fuzzy from the whisky. "What are you talking about?"

Shay downed the rest of his drink. "The zoo, man. The bigfoot is heading toward the Bronx Zoo!"

CHAPTER TWENTY-FIVE

Shay fired up his app and got a car for them that was only two minutes away. The police had the Fordham Station taped off. The crowds had grown so thick, it looked like the exterior of Yankee Stadium after a playoff win.

A man wearing a turban was having a heated discussion with an elderly Jamaican man outside the bar.

"I'm telling you, it's a bigfoot!" the man with the turban said passionately.

The Jamaican man rolled his eyes and put his hand up. "Man, you're crazy. There's no such thing as bigfoot."

Turban man held up his cell phone and played a video. "Are you blind? What do you see?"

"Some crazy guy in a costume."

"Look at its face! Who would make a costume of a bigfoot that looked beaten up?"

At that moment, three teens dressed as rotted zombies strolled past them, toking on their vape pens.

The Jamaican guy smiled. "Maybe it's a zombie bigfoot costume."

"Pshaw! There's no such thing as a zombie bigfoot."

"Or a non-zombie bigfoot."

Shay spotted the car and tapped Vito on the chest. Before he got inside, he said to the Jamaican man, "He's right, you know."

"Who the fuck asked you?" they said in unison.

Vito clambered in next to Shay in the back seat. "God, I love this city."

The driver was a twenty-ish woman with beaded cornrows and quite a few facial piercings. "Wow, this is crazy," she said, making a difficult U-turn around the L pillar and gawkers. "You guys want water? You can plug in your phone and play your own music if you want."

"We're good. Just need to get to the zoo as quickly as possible," Shay said. He wished he'd brought a whisky to go.

"I got you. You know the zoo is closed, right?"

Vito leaned forward and said, "We're meeting someone there."

Naturally, they hit every red light. Shay muttered, "Come the fuck on," every time they had to stop. His skin was starting to itch. This was going to take forever.

"Is there any way we can get off this road?" Shay asked the driver.

She tapped at her phone's screen in its cradle. "Sorry, but I have to follow the map my company gives."

"You live in the Bronx?" Shay asked.

"All my life," she said with pride.

"Then you must know a dozen better routes to the zoo." He took his wallet out and reached behind the window where he kept his license. Behind it was his emergency fifty-dollar bill. When he was in college, that fifty was broken out to cover bar tabs. As an adult, he'd never had to use it. He took the old, creased fifty and put it on the center armrest. "Will a cash tip get you to forget the frigging map?"

She palmed the bill and took a hard left. Vito slid across the seat and pressed into Shay.

"If you can ignore red lights, there's more for you," Vito said.

"And step on it!"

The car accelerated, flying through a busy intersection.

"Step on it?" Vito whispered to Shay.

"I've always wanted to say that. When am I going to get another chance?"

It didn't take long for Shay to regret giving away his fifty. Their driver must have gotten her license from NASCAR. She drove like a demon, just missing pedestrians, cars, a mailbox and a light pole, blowing past red lights with glee. At one point, he swore he heard her give a maniacal giggle as she swerved around a woman pushing a shopping cart filled with bulging black trash bags.

Shay and Vito buckled up and gripped the handholds above the windows.

A pair of cop cars whizzed past them, oblivious to her insane feats of driving.

Next thing Shay knew, the car was coming to a skidding stop beside the Rockefeller Fountain. Beyond the fountain was the entrance to the zoo.

The driver clapped her hands and whooped. "Damn, that was fun!"

Vito's hand shook as he pulled out a pair of twenties. "Thanks for the ride."

"You should consider a career in drag racing," Shay said as he exited the car.

"You really think so?" She pulled away, laying rubber on the parking lot's pavement.

The zoo beyond the gates was dark, but they could hear the barking of the sea lions and caw of birds. The night itself was alive with the wailing of police sirens, the air filled with the steady chop of helicopters.

"Are you sure about this?" Vito said.

"Kind of."

"Where do you think it'll go?"

"I would say the gorilla forest, but I think that's all enclosed and it might not be able to get inside." He had been to the zoo once with Caitlin and Katie this summer but had been too absorbed in the Yankee game on his phone to remember that whole Congo setup.

"Unless it breaks its way in and lets the gorillas out."

They made their way up and over the front gate with less ease than it would have been ten years earlier. The police sirens sounded as if they were getting closer. A helicopter took up residence in a patch of sky over the zoo.

"Looks like I was right," Shay said.

"And it looks like we beat it here. It's either coming through that gate or the bison enclosure. Maybe we should split up."

"No way. Everyone who splits up dies apart in the movies. Not gonna happen. I say we wait right here. The helicopters will tell us what direction to go now."

They walked through a grassy quadrangle. Exotic birds answered the call of the whirling copters.

"Birds of prey over there," Vito pointed. "Guess they don't like the sound of the choppers."

"Have you been moonlighting at the zoo without telling me?"

"Danielle got one of those yearly passes. We've brought Meredith here about ten times so far. We just do little bits at a time."

The rattling of the front gate stopped them cold. They spun on their heels. Shay felt adrenaline power through his system.

A huge, dark figure shook the gate for a moment before it scrabbled up and over.

Shay and Vito ran behind a tree so the bigfoot couldn't see them.

The moment the bigfoot touched upon the grass, its limp grew a little less pronounced. It sniffed the air, looking around with its hands still clenched into fists. Shay watched its posture begin to relax. It made an almost affectionate cooing sound as it walked.

"Jesus, it sounds happy," Vito whispered.

That's because it is, Shay thought. *Coming here is the best thing to happen to it since I decided to take it home to make a fast buck. I'm the fucking monster, not you, big guy. If I thought you'd understand me, I'd tell you how sorry I am.*

Not that he was going to attempt to do such a thing. He was pretty sure if the bigfoot spotted him, it would be beating him with his own severed arms in seconds.

It sounded like an army of police were just a minute or so away. This respite from the insanity wouldn't last long.

The wind shifted and the barking of the sea lions intensified. Even they knew the bigfoot had arrived.

The sasquatch stopped for a moment and cocked its head toward the sea lion exhibit that wasn't too far ahead. Shay gripped the tree trunk as if he needed it to ground him before being sucked into a tornado. Vito breathed heavily onto the back of his neck. He normally would have told him to give him some space, but he didn't dare make a sound.

When the sasquatch resumed walking, Shay and Vito crept to the next tree, keeping the beast in their sights.

Red lights lit up the night. The cops had arrived. A strong spotlight searched the grounds until it settled on the bigfoot. "It's in there!" a woman called out.

The bigfoot turned and held its arm over its face to protect its eye from the brilliant light. Another spotlight from above found it, too.

Snarling at the sky, the bigfoot staggered toward the sea lions. The closer it got, the more excited the sea lions became. The birds of prey enclosure burst at the seams with cries. In the distance, lions roared and an elephant bellowed.

The entire zoo came alive. Shay knew they were all properly caged, but the little shred of safety he'd felt quickly melted away.

Police swarmed over the gate like ants heading for a picnic.

They couldn't hide anymore. Shay knew it was crazy, but it was time to do something.

He popped out from behind the tree and faced the oncoming army of police. Shay was instantly blinded by dozens of flashlight beams.

"It's okay," he said, knowing how supremely stupid that sounded.

"Put your hands up, now!"

Shay did as he was told. Vito came out from behind the tree with his hands up.

"You don't have to shoot it," Vito said.

The police ran for them. Shay turned around and saw the bigfoot hop the low fence that surrounded the sea lion display. It hit the water-filled moat with a tremendous splash. The sea lions went wild.

"Come on," he said to Vito, lowering his arms and running to the sea lion exhibit.

"Stop right now!"

Vito ran beside him. Shay had a hard time getting his wind, but his legs felt infused with newfound strength. He kept waiting to get shot in the back.

They were close.

The sea lions sounded terrified.

I know how you feel!

They were closer.

Closer.

The bigfoot had a difficult time getting out of the water. Because of its body mass, it had never been a good swimmer. It would wade up to its legs in rivers and lakes to drink or catch fish with its bare hands. But after the time it had been swallowed by a flash flood and almost drowned, it had been terrified of going any deeper than that in water.

This water smelled funny and was very cold. The sasquatch fought desperately to find a handhold on the steep, hard surface. Something heavy and solid brushed against its back. The bigfoot slapped the surface of the water, missing whatever it had been.

Fear of the water made it forget all of its hurts and pains.

It sank to the bottom, arms desperately reaching for the surface.

Crouching down, it sprang up as hard and fast as it could. Water rocketed like a geyser as the bigfoot broke free. It hit its chest onto a rocky surface and clung with all its might, terrified of going back under.

Pulling itself out of the moat, it stayed on all fours, trying to collect itself.

Strange creatures bounced and rolled before it, making harsh noises. It didn't speak their language, but it knew they were afraid and angry and wanted it to go away.

The bigfoot grumbled back at them, though it had little strength to muster up a good and proper warning to leave it alone.

This was not home. The stink water was in its nose, messing up its senses. It couldn't tell where it should go from here.

It looked up into the light from the sky. Why was it there? The light made the bigfoot uneasy. It much preferred the dark. Why couldn't it find the dark in this place?

It needed to find home.

Pulling itself up, it climbed up the rocks until it made it to the top. The sasquatch stood tall and roared, wanting everything to stop making so much noise and light and go away.

CHAPTER TWENTY-SIX

"I'm sorry I'm a fucking idiot," Shay said to Vito as he ran. It sounded like the bigfoot and the sea lions were not getting along.

"It's okay," Vito said. "I'm used to it."

Shay thought there had to be someone working at the zoo who had heard the commotion by now. He hoped they had access to a proper tranquilizer gun and would subdue the bigfoot. His and Vito's job was to stop the police from shooting the beast.

They both had to put their hands out and grab the iron rail around the sea lion exhibit to stop themselves. The bigfoot was perched on top of the rocks, making a hell of a racket. It did not sound happy. The sea lions were going between lying on the rocks and dipping into the water. All of them were making equally unsettling noises. Shay could barely hear himself think over it.

It didn't help that four helicopters hovered overhead and a battalion of angry cops were upon them.

Can't believe our best case scenario is to get arrested.

"Get down on the ground!" several cops ordered them. Others were shouting things that Shay couldn't understand over the roar of beast and man's machinery.

A large sea lion exploded out of the water, bellied to the rocks below the bigfoot and loosed a barked that sounded like a challenge.

You picked the wrong time to get territorial, Shay thought, watching the sea lion. The flash of anger that lit up the sasquatch's face made Shay cringe.

The bigfoot stopped its own cries and peered down at the sea lion.

Shay watched open-mouthed as the creature jumped onto the sea lion's back. It bit down on the sea lion's neck. The sea lion let out a howl that would stay with Shay until he took his last breath. It undulated over the rocks, heading for the water with the bigfoot attached to its back.

The police were all around him and Vito, staring at the insane spectacle. The bigfoot and the sea lion thrashed in the water, driving all of the other sea lions onto the rocks. As the water turned red and frothy from their struggles, the cops pulled out their guns and followed the melee.

Without thinking what he was doing, Shay hopped over the rail and put his body between at least some of the guns and the battling creatures. "Please, don't shoot! Get someone to tranquilize them. Now!"

Quite a few, "Get the fuck out of there," commands were sent his way.

Vito joined him on the wrong side of the rail. "You're gonna have to shoot us both."

Shay didn't like the sound of that. These cops looked just scared enough to do it by accident.

A few cops grabbed for them. Shay stepped back and his foot slipped. He reached out for Vito to keep from falling.

Instead, he dragged them both into the roiling moat.

Fishy water filled his mouth and slithered up his nostrils. For a moment, he thought he was going to drown.

Then the bigfoot and sea lion collided with him and he swam like a man possessed. He'd stop to find a way to pull himself up, fail, and resume swimming in a circle. It felt as if the angry creatures were following him, intent on bringing him into their brawl.

Police shouted at them to get out of the water.

Easier said than done!

Shay's clothes got heavier as they absorbed the foul water. He kicked as hard as he could, but his shoulders and arms were starting to tire. From the look and sound of it, Vito's were, too.

He turned around when he heard a great tearing sound. He wished he hadn't. The bigfoot had pulled half the flesh from the sea lion's face. It flopped like an empty mask on the side of its snout. But still the sea lion swam, the bigfoot riding it like a horse. They bashed Shay and Vito as the sea lion made a mad dash around the moat. All of Shay's air exploded from his burning lungs and he nearly lost consciousness.

A hand appeared in front of his face. It was Vito. He'd somehow made it onto the rocks.

"I've got you!" Vito said.

He was surrounded by agitated sea lions.

Shay lunged for his hand at the same moment an angry sea lion nudged Vito back into the moat. This was also a second before the dying sea lion glided right into them, driving them under.

Sinking fast, Shay looked up to see the massive shadow pass overhead. So many lights were cast on the exhibit now, it might as well have been daytime.

He saw Vito beside him. His eyes were closed and it looked like he'd been knocked out. Shay grabbed onto him and swam for the surface. He broke through, gasping. Holding Vito under his arm, he fought to keep his friend's head above water.

"I need help!" Shay sputtered. Talking was a bad idea as more water tinged with fish and now sea lion blood went down his throat.

There were splashes all around him.

A half-dozen cops selflessly dove in to save them, working together to get Shay and Vito on the rocks. They fired their guns in the air to chase the sea lions away from them.

Lying on his back, gasping, Shay thought their plan had worked. Someone from the zoo was surely there now with a rifle loaded with a heavy-duty tranquilizer.

Then, against the backdrop of the light from the helicopters, Shay saw the bigfoot clambering back on top of the rocks. It glowered at him with one hate-filled eye, a struggling sea lion in its grasp.

In that brief moment their eyes locked, Shay knew exactly what it was thinking.

You did this to me. You brought me here to this hell. And now you're going to hell with me!

Maybe it was a stretch anthropomorphizing it that way, and maybe it was Shay projecting his own feelings onto the creature, but deep down, he knew he was right.

Shots rang out just as the bigfoot swung the helpless sea lion over its head. The sasquatch fell backwards and out of sight a hair before the sea lion came hurtling toward them.

Shay pushed the cop attending to him into the water and just managed to roll his unconscious friend out of the way before it felt like a building fell on top of him and he felt no more.

CHAPTER TWENTY-SEVEN

Vito held tight to Danielle's hand.

When she'd seen what had happened on the news, the video capturing EMTs putting Vito on a stretcher, all of her anger had turned to fear. It had taken her some time to find the hospital they'd brought him to. She'd been there at his bedside when he finally regained consciousness. Vito couldn't think of a more beautiful face to come back from what he thought was his death.

After crying and hugging him, she'd called for the doctor.

In seconds, Vito was the most popular patient on the floor, judging by all the attention he got. It was all overwhelming. He reached out for Danielle and asked, "Where's Shay?"

A nurse bustled his wife aside to check his IV.

The rest of the night was a blur. He'd fallen asleep again after hearing a doctor talk to Danielle about a concussion.

The next couple of days were no picnic. Detectives came to question him about what had happened at the zoo and the subway. They were very curious to know why he and Shay had been following the man.

"That was no man," Vito said.

"Yes, it was. His name was Paul Hibbard, a Gulf War vet with severe psychological issues. We're not sure why he put on that costume and did what he did. I'm sure toxicology will reveal he was on some heavy duty drugs. PCP most likely. We'll probably never know what set him off. You're lucky to be alive. Especially considering how close you two were to him the entire night."

Vito said nothing more after that. This was all just a big snow job. He claimed memory loss and his doctor backed him up, telling the detectives that it could be temporary or permanent. Only time would tell.

Then came the calls from reporters. Vito didn't even grace them with a 'no comment'. If it was possible, he just wanted to truly forget everything.

Until that one visitor came to his room.

Now he was alone with Danielle in his home, on their couch, with Meredith in the kitchen doing her homework. A normal day. But what he had to tell her was anything but.

To her credit, she took it all in, asking a few questions here or there. He felt like crying when she took his hand and said, "I believe you, honey. Are you sure you want to do this?"

"No. But it feels like I have to. I owe it. Big time."

"All right. I'm not crazy about this, but I'll stand behind you. As long as you never lie to me again."

He kissed her softly. "I promise."

They went to Montefiore Hospital and asked to see Katie. She was fortunately on a break in the ER. The receptionist paged her and she came out to meet them. She looked tired, five years older than she had on Halloween.

"Look at you up and about," she said to Vito as she hugged Danielle and then him. "How's your head feeling?"

"Like Aaron Judge used it for batting practice."

"The headaches will go away."

"That's what the doctor says."

"You want to go?" Katie asked.

"If we could."

They followed Katie to the employee elevator and got out on the fourth floor. Katie greeted nurses and doctors she knew as they walked down the corridor. Vito saw people sleeping in their beds, some hooked up to tubes and wires. Others sat in chairs, happily chatting with their visitors. He hated the smell of hospitals. Who didn't?

They turned into room 121. An old man with a week's worth of stubble stared at the television, seemingly unaware they had entered the room.

On the other side of the curtain, Shay lay in bed covered in enough casts to qualify him as a mummy. When he saw them, his eyes lit up.

"They said you were alive but I told them you'd been brain dead for years," he said to Vito. It was the first time they'd met since that night, what with Vito being in a different hospital and contending with everything since.

Katie had told him that Shay also had a concussion, along with a broken pelvis, five broken ribs, a fractured leg and arm and broken nose. If the sea lion had landed on him just a little more to the left, there would have been nothing left of him to patch up.

Brushing Shay's forehead tenderly, Katie said, "How are you feeling?"

"Good until those magic meds wear off."

"You want some ginger ale?"

"I'd kill for one. Or a Guinness if there's one stashed in the nurse's fridge."

Katie smiled. "In your dreams. I'll be right back."

"I'll come with you," Danielle said and they both popped out of the room.

"You look like shit," Vito said.

"I'm hoping to work my way up to feeling like shit. How are you?"

"Head hurts, but it's fine." Vito pulled up a chair. "I told Danielle the truth."

Shay nodded. "I did the same with Katie."

"How'd it go?"

"She says she believes me. I think she's working hard at convincing herself she does."

"Well, the rest of the world thinks it was this Paul Hibbard dude hopped up on drugs."

"I saw. Fucking liars. Fake news is right. I'll bet there never was a Paul Hibbard to begin with."

Vito chuckled. "Yeah, right. What kind of a name is Hibbard?"

Even though officials had blamed it all on this mystery Hibbard man, social media was on fire with hundreds of pictures and videos of the bigfoot during its long, horrid night in the Bronx. The words 'conspiracy' and 'bigfoot' were trending hot and heavy.

Shay tried to shift in the bed, resulting in a pained hiss and a few choice expletives.

"Someone came to meet me at the hospital the other day," Vito said.

"Was it that stripper I sent? Hope he was fat."

"I'm serious. He's a cryptozoologist. I checked him out and he's legit. He's written a bunch of books about bigfoot.

Been on TV. He's even in the process of opening up a museum."

Shay grew wary. "What did you tell him?"

"The truth. He knew right away that the press was lying. Said he'd seen sasquatches before in the woods of New York. He wants us to show him where we found it."

"Why?"

"He thinks there has to be more than one out there."

Shay shook his head. "No way. I'm not creating another circus just to watch another one of those poor things get killed."

Vito leaned back in the chair. "He doesn't want that either. His goal is to find them and study them. Find ways to protect them."

"That bigfoot did a pretty good job on its own until we came along."

"Actually, you're wrong. We're not the ones who darted it. If there are more, they could be in danger."

Shay's eyes wandered to the ceiling. He chewed on his upper lip, silent.

"He said he'll pay us a hundred grand," Vito added.

Shay nearly bolted up in bed, the instant agony making him cry out, "Jesus, Mary and Joseph just kill me now!"

When he settled down, he said, "A hundred grand?"

"Yep."

Katie and Danielle walked back into the room, talking in hushed tones.

Shay looked at Vito. "When do we go?"

CHAPTER TWENTY-EIGHT

Sheridan Barnard scratched at an itch he couldn't reach with a ruler. His trailer was colder than a well digger's ass. All the extra layers of Goodwill clothes he'd pulled from the donation bins made scratching harder than it needed to be.

Belching after taking a swig of beer, he patted his rumbling stomach.

"I know, I know. Don't get your panties in a twist."

Donning a wool coat that was missing all but one button, he stepped outside and pulled it around his chest, fighting the bitter cold wind that came up and slapped him. Trudging down the worn path, he mumbled about moving to Florida next winter. He was getting too old for these ice-cold winters.

A couple of weeks back, he'd bartered with a farmer – a week's work for some cash and a couple of chickens and a rooster. The cash was for beer and bread and toilet paper. The chickens, well, he needed them to keep him in eggs and later, meat. He'd hoped to get another week out of the farmer and some more chickens, but two were better than none.

Right now, he could go for some sunny side up eggs. The slate sky threatened snow. Just what he needed.

Rounding the bend, he expected to hear some clucking.

What he got was a vision of three dead animals, all of them missing their heads.

The heat of his anger fought and won against the cold.

"Goddamn squatches!"

The End

Check out other great

Cryptid Novels!

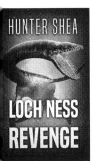

Hunter Shea

LOCH NESS REVENGE

Deep in the murky waters of Loch Ness, the creature known as Nessie has returned. Twins Natalie and Austin McQueen watched in horror as their parents were devoured by the world's most infamous lake monster. Two decades later, it's their turn to hunt the legend. But what lurks in the Loch is not what they expected. Nessie is devouring everything in and around the Loch, and it's not alone. Hell has come to the Scottish Highlands. In a fierce battle between man and monster, the world may never be the same. Praise for THEY RISE : "Outrageous, balls to the wall...made me yearn for 3D glasses and a tub of popcorn, extra butter!" – The Eyes of Madness "A fast-paced, gore-heavy splatter fest of sharksploitation." The Werd "A rocket paced horror story. I enjoyed the hell out of this book." Shotgun Logic Reviews

C.G. Mosley

BAKER COUNTY BIGFOOT CHRONICLE

Marie Bledsoe only wants her missing brother Kurt back. She'll stop at nothing to make it happen and, with the help of Kurt's friend Tony, along with Sheriff Ray Cochran, Marie embarks on a terrifying journey deep into the belly of the mysterious Walker Laboratory to find him. However, what she and her companions find lurking in the laboratory basement is beyond comprehension. There are cryptids from the forest being held captive there and something...else. Enjoy this suspenseful tale from the mind of C.G. Mosley, author of Wood Ape. Welcome back to Baker County, a place where monsters do lurk in the night!

Check out other great

Cryptid Novels!

P.K. Hawkins

THE CRYPTID FILES

Fresh out of the academy with top marks, Agent Bradley Tennyson is expecting to have the pick of cases and investigations throughout the country. So he's shocked when instead he is assigned as the new partner to "The Crag," an agent well past his prime. He thinks the assignment is a punishment. It's anything but. Agent George Crag has been doing this job for far longer than most, and he knows what skeletons his bosses have in the closet and where the bodies are buried. He has pretty much free reign to pick his cases and he knows exactly which one he wants to use to break in his new young partner: the disappearance and murder of a couple of college kids in a remote mountain town. Tennyson doesn't realize it, but Crag is about to introduce him to a world he never believed existed: The Cryptid Files, a world of strange monsters roaming in the night. Because these murders have been going on for a long time, and evidence is mounting that the murderer may just in fact be the legendary Bigfoot.

Gerry Griffiths

DOWN FROM BEAST MOUNTAIN

A beast with a grudge has come down from the mountain to terrorize the townsfolk of Porterville. The once sleepy town is suddenly wide awake. Sheriff Abel McGuire and game warden Grant Tanner frantically investigate one brutal slaying after another as they follow the blood trail they hope will eventually lead to the monstrous killer. But they better hurry and stop the carnage before the census taker has to come out and change the population sign on the edge of town to ZERO.

Check out other great

Cryptid Novels!

Hunter Shea

THE DOVER DEMON

The Dover Demon is real...and it has returned. In 1977, Sam Brogna and his friends came upon a terrifying, alien creature on a deserted country road. What they witnessed was so bizarre, so chilling, they swore their silence. But their lives were changed forever. Decades later, the town of Dover has been hit by a massive blizzard. Sam's son, Nicky, is drawn to search for the infamous cryptid, only to disappear into the bowels of a secret underground lair. The Dover Demon is far deadlier than anyone could have believed. And there are many of them. Can Sam and his reunited friends rescue Nicky and battle a race of creatures so powerful, so sinister, that history itself has been shaped by their secretive presence? "THE DOVER DEMON is Shea's most delightful and insidiously terrifying monster yet." – Shotgun Logic Reviews "An excellent horror novel and a strong standout in the UFO and cryptid subgenres." –Hellnotes "Non-stop action awaits those brave enough to dive into the small town of Dover, and if you're lucky, you won't see the Demon himself!" – The Scary Reviews PRAISE FOR SWAMP MONSTER MASSACRE "B-horror movie fans rejoice, Hunter Shea is here to bring you the ultimate tale of terror!" – Horror Novel Reviews "A nonstop thrill ride! I couldn't put this book down." – Cedar Hollow Horror Reviews

Armand Rosamilia

THE BEAST

The end of summer, 1986. With only a few days left until the new school year, twins Jeremy and Jack Schaffer are on very different paths. Jeremy is the geek, playing Dungeons & Dragons with friends Kathleen and Randy, while Jack is the jock, getting into trouble with his buddies. And then everything changes when neighbor Mister Higgins is killed by a wild animal in his yard. Was it a bear? There's something big lurking in the woods behind their New Jersey home. Will the police be able to solve the murder before more Middletown residents are ripped apart?

Check out other great

Cryptid Novels!

Edward J. McFadden III

THE CRYPTID CLUB

When cryptozoologist Ash Cohn receives a gold embossed printed invitation inviting him to join The Cryptid Club, he sees the resolution to all his problems.Famous cryptid scientist and biologist, Lester Treemont, one of the world's richest men, and the leader of the Cryptid Club, is dying. What he offers via his invitation is a chance to succeed him. To take over his wealth, laboratory, and discoveries. All Ash has to do is beat eight others like him in a series of tests both mental and physical involving Treemont's collection of cryptids. Seems simple enough, and Ash has nothing to lose.Nine strangers from across the globe, all with reasons for wanting to win. When they start dying one by one, the competition shifts to one of survival. Who among them will rise to the top and reign over The Cryptid Club?

William Meikle

INFESTATION

It was supposed to be a simple mission. A suspected Russian spy boat is in trouble in Canadian waters. Investigate and report are the orders. But when Captain John Banks and his squad arrive, it is to find an empty vessel, and a scene of bloody mayhem. Soon they are in a fight for their lives, for there are things in the icy seas off Baffin Island, scuttling, hungry things with a taste for human flesh. They are swarming. And they are growing. "Scotland's best Horror writer" Ginger Nuts of Horror "The premier storyteller of our time." - Famous Monsters of Filmland

Made in the USA
Las Vegas, NV
18 May 2021

23289102R00104